PLEASE DON'T READ
UNLESS I'M DEAD

GRAHAM HALL

Bretan Palace

© 2024 by Graham Hall

ISBN-13: 979-8-9901098-1-0 pbk.
ISBN-13: 979-8-9901098-0-3 digital

Library of Congress Control Number: 2024903503

Cover Design by Adam Hay Studio

Bretan Palace

For my lovely wife and three amazing daughters.

Also, special thanks to my mom and sister for the invaluable advice throughout this process.

CONTENTS

CONTENTS

PREFACE

It seems like you cannot read a news article, turn on the television, or listen to the radio these days without being bombarded with talk of Artificial Intelligence (A.I.). But the concept of A.I. is nothing new, as the idea of it has been around since the 1950's. I distinctly remember that several of the movies and TV shows I watched as a kid in the early 1990's focused entire plotlines on the subject. For shows like the *Star Trek* series, A.I. was generally portrayed in a positive light, providing humans with a necessary tool that allowed them to explore the universe.

However, movies like *The Terminator* presented A.I. in a much darker light, as something to be feared, and which, when given power and control over weapons (a questionable decision but needed to drive the plot), could spell the end of mankind. Even *Star Trek: The Next Generation*, which had a physical display of A.I. in the beloved android, Data, as a main character, showcased the possible negative aspect of A.I. when the show introduced Data's malevolent brother, Lore, and the series' most frightening and daunting villain—the Borg. And for a while, that is where A.I. remained for the majority of the world, a concept that often played out on the screen or in books, but never in real life.

That was, until 2022, when ChatGPT and other services made A.I. available to the public, and ignited a storm of debate and curiosity, part of which inspired this story. However, while the uses of A.I. formed the skeleton of the idea for this story, it was not used in any part for creating the story you are about to read. No, all words and ideas, whether good, bad, or ugly, are from a human—either from my painfully slow typing and scattered brain or from family members, who added significant improve-ments to the text I drafted.

Now before we get to the story, I should make the following statements. The story you are about to read is fictional, all characters and events, however poorly written, are made up and do not describe an actual person, people, incident, proceeding or occurrences. Further, this story is purely for entertainment purposes and does not constitute legal advice. Readers should not act upon nor accept the details in this story as factual or accurate representations of the law, including legal procedure. I hope you enjoy!

DINNER CONVERSATION

The room had become almost entirely dark, save for the light coming off the computer screen which illuminated the olive-colored complexion of Jamal's face. He had been sitting at the lightweight walnut-colored IKEA table for over two hours, well after the sun had set, and with it the room emptying of light. Immediately after his arrival home from work that day, he started typing the email.

The email itself was easy—the words just flowed from him with ease, as he had been mulling over the message for the past week. But the act of sending it, that was some-thing else. He sat alone in the dark, not even realizing day had turned into dusk then into pitch black night, as he agonized about what to do. He sat gazing, as if paralyzed, at the little rectangular blue "send" button, which seemingly taunted him to click it. He had come close to doing it right after typing the last words, but then was stopped by the fear of what would happen next. And so he sat, not moving, gazing at the screen in the dark.

Around seven thirty, the silence was interrupted by the sound of a key turning in the front door lock of the two-bedroom apartment. Jamal heard the door slowly open, then close, turning his head to peer at the light which shone through the room's partially open door. He took a couple of deep breaths, at the same time felt sweat pooling under his arms and his heart starting to race. Taking a final deep breath and slowly exhaling, he said to himself "screw it" as he pressed the blue button. His rapid heartbeats subsided, replaced by longer, stronger beats he could distinctly hear as he rubbed his palms over his closed eyes and forehead. "Oh well, that's done" he thought to himself as he stood up from the chair. He could feel the blood rushing back into his calves as he gingerly walked over to the door leading from the dark room into the brightly lit hallway.

"Oh, hi, I didn't know you were home," Marguerite said with a warm smile.

"Yes, sorry, I've been home for a while now," Jamal said as he stretched his back, which had become tight and sore from sitting motionless for so long.

"Oh, were you just sitting in the office in the dark?" she asked. "What were you doing in there?"

"Nothing, um nothing at all, just looking at some stuff I guess," he responded.

"Well, did you at least make dinner?" she asked half seriously, knowing the response was most likely no.

"Umm, no, no I didn't," he replied as he looked around the hallway, trying to avoid making direct eye contact with her as his eyes adjusted to the light.

"I figured," Marguerite scoffed, briefly walking toward Jamal before turning right toward the kitchen located opposite of the room where Jamal had been sitting.

The two had known each other for years and she was

accustomed to his aloofness. They had originally met while both were students at the University of North Carolina, Charlotte, or UNC Charlotte (UNCC) as it was often referred. She was an undergrad studying chemistry with hopes of going to medical school, while he was earning his master's in accounting. During the fall semester of her sophomore year, Marguerite was invited one night to a meeting of the African Nations Students Association, which she reluctantly attended. After almost an hour of standing alone in a corner, Jamal finally approached her.

They immediately bonded over being the only North Africans in the room. The bonding continued as they engaged in a conversation about their mutual light skin tone, something which they felt made them stand out in the room that night. And while the people at the event could not have been more welcoming and warmer to them, they each felt it deep down—a feeling of not truly belonging. Each was accustomed to people assuming they were from someplace else. Marguerite, with her wavy dark brunette hair and grayish-green eyes, often heard people comment that she must be Greek. For Jamal, the assumption was that he was Middle Eastern, with Saudi Arabia being the most common country guessed. They each had shared in the experience of having to defend their heritage when people stared at them questioningly at hearing them say they were African. However, when Jamal learned Marguerite did not speak Arabic, he began teasing her, cracking jokes about her upbringing.

While Marguerite did not appreciate the jokes, she could tell—at least she thought—from his face there was no ill will or malice behind them. In fact, there were seemingly no discernable emotions at all. It was this mystery of who he was, what he felt, that drew her to him. As the ribbing continued, she felt the need to defend herself. She told Jamal that while her father was Moroccan, her mother was French and she had been raised splitting time between Lyons, France and the United States, with only a couple of trips to Morocco to visit distant relatives. Jamal did not seem to care for her backstory and stated it was no excuse for not knowing Arabic. As her feelings of anger rose, Marguerite began to curse Jamal in French, eventually saying something along the lines that she hoped one day he would go back home and die with the other terrorists—a statement she instantly regretted making. After saying this, she turned away from him and started to walk toward the main door when she heard Jamal say in recognizable, albeit poorly worded, French: "si tel est ton souhait, qu'il en soit ainsi" (if that is your wish, so be it).

Shocked by his response, Marguerite immediately turned to face him and to her surprise, rather than seeing a grin or smirk on his face, there was nothing. She walked back to him and asked if he understood what she had said. He replied coldly that he had, and then, after a pause, told her with a slight smile that he knew more than just two languages. Based on their prior conversation, she assumed he meant this in jest, and felt the blood flowing from her hands as her face turned red in embarrassment. Immediately she profusely apologized for her comment, claiming that was not a reflection of her beliefs. Jamal did not seem to be too offended and told her to just let it go.

After pausing to calm down, they began to chat about school, music, and things to do around Charlotte. The conversation continued until close to midnight and, as the night came to a close, they exchanged phone numbers. For the next two years, they spent a considerable amount of time together, going to concerts, dining at local restaurants, and taking trips to the nearby U.S. National Whitewater Center. They visited Lake Norman, the mountains, and the beaches outside Charleston, South Carolina. While they at times jokingly discussed dating; in fact many of their friends thought they were a couple, they never did end up getting together during this time. They remained friends after graduation, keeping in constant contact, despite Marguerite moving to Boston to attend medical school, Jamal remained in Charlotte, where he worked as an accountant at South Lake Union Management Corporation.

Seven years later, with medical school and her residency complete, Marguerite returned to Charlotte to work at a small clinic near the South Park neighborhood. Upon her return, their friendship seemingly picked up right where it left off seven years before. But as the days turned to weeks, their feelings for each other grew in a new direction, to the point where one day, Jamal finally asked her out on a formal date. Eventually, this led to the mutual decision to move in together.

Jamal rubbed his eyes again before turning around and walking into the living room located at the center of their apartment. He stood in the middle of the room, looking at the couch and debating whether to sit down or not. He felt odd in that moment, as he gazed at the beige sectional couch. He knew his body was standing in the room, but he felt lost, as though he was not really present in the room. His thoughts, which only a couple of hours ago had been laser focused, were now jumbled and distant.

"Are you good with buttered chicken and rice?" asked Marguerite, as she looked at Jamal from the other side of the counter which separated the living room from the kitchen.

Jamal nodded absently in the affirmative, still trying to decide what to do next, his mind seemingly miles away. After a minute or so of standing motionless in the living room with his eyes focused blankly on the couch, he turned and walked back into the dark office. He sat back down in front of the computer, moving the mouse to un-lock the screen in the process. He paused for a moment before moving the cursor to the top left of the screen, where he clicked on the *Inbox* icon. His email immediately refreshed; however, there were no new messages. "What did you expect," a distant voice in his head echoed. Jamal shook his head and then rubbed his strained eyes again. He sat there silently for a few moments before clicking on the *Inbox* icon. He repeated this same routine, with the same result, for the next twenty minutes before the routine was finally interrupted by Marguerite yelling "dinner's ready" which resonated throughout the small apartment.

Jamal looked at his desktop, scanning all of the items strewn across it. He first looked at his brown leather wallet, then at the crumpled white envelope, then at the ID badge next to it before he finally focused on the black metallic handgun sitting on the edge of the desk. His mind went back to the moment he had asked his cousin to get the gun for him. It was at a time of great uncertainty in his life, when he was newly arrived in the country and feared that there were those out there who would want to harm him. This was not just because of to whom he was related, but also because of his identity at a time only a few months after the terrorist attacks of September 11th. In those first few weeks after arrival in this country, he decided the risk of having a gun, which probably was not legal, was less than the risk of not having one at all. He chuckled a little at how irrational and even naïve his reasoning was back then. Looking back at the computer screen, he thought how the gun may just end up saving his life. Finally, he stood up from his chair and left the office.

As Jamal re-entered the living room, he could see that Marguerite had already set down two plates full of buttered chicken, rice, and cauliflower on the counter. She was back in the kitchen, pouring a glass of wine for herself and a glass of iced tea for him. He sat down on the Pottery Barn counter stool closet to the wall, and for the first time noticed the enticing aroma of garlic, ginger, and coriander emanating from the familiar reddish orange sauce surrounding the chicken. The delicious smells, which caused Jamal's stomach to grumble with hunger, momentarily distracted him from the thoughts which had occupied him ever since he arrived home that night.

"Smells great," he said as Marguerite sat down next to him.

"Thanks. I tried something a little different, using those whole tomatoes that were sitting in the fridge, rather than from a can," Marguerite replied.

"Well, it definitely works, it tastes great," Jamal said with his mouth half full of chicken.

"Glad to hear," Marguerite responded with a smile. "So how was your day?"

"Eh, it was a day," Jamal replied curtly after swallow-ing the chicken. "How was yours?" he asked, as manners would dictate, but more important to him at that moment was to shift the subject to anything other than his job.

"It wasn't bad, a little bit busy in the afternoon as we were down a nurse who had some family emergency and didn't come in, but we managed."

"Oh," Jamal replied, still partially distracted, and wondering if anyone had yet read what he sent and, if so, had they responded.

"Yes, it was a bit annoying. I feel behind schedule this morning and couldn't catch up," Marguerite continued. "And of course, some of the patients were clearly irritated and upset with having to wait to be seen, but I mean there was nothing we could do. I tried telling some of them we had someone out, but I don't think any of them cared."

"Yeah, no doubt," Jamal replied instinctually, still not fully paying attention to her. He could feel both of his legs shaking from jitters as he sat in the chair, and he wondered if she had noticed them moving. It didn't seem like she had, or at least she hadn't thought enough of it to say anything at this point.

"So how about you," Marguerite asked. "Are you liking the new job?"

"Um, it's fine, I guess."

"Are the people on your team nice?"

"Well, um, they aren't," he started, before pausing as he tried to shift his thoughts from the email he had sent, back to the conversation. "The people on the team don't really talk, at least they don't talk to me. I don't get the feeling that they are all that warm, especially when it comes to me."

"Oh," she replied with some surprise. She paused for a moment, debating whether to move on to another subject or continue pressing him on what was bothering him. "Is it because of your background, Sudanese and Mus-lim?"

"It could be, I can't say for sure," he responded.

"And it wouldn't have anything to do with your uncle, would it?"

"I doubt it," he replied. "I don't think anyone there even knows who Omar is, and even if they did, I highly doubt they would know he is my uncle."

"Well, that's good," Marguerite said, trying to move the conversation in a more positive   direction. "It is just a job, you can always look for another one, but it was a good thing that Alex was able to get you the position."

"Yes, that is true," Jamal said. "Working in audit isn't exactly what I thought I'd be doing with my career, but it is better than being laid off and unemployed, I guess."

"Yes, it certainly is," Marguerite agreed, trying to reassure Jamal. After a short pause, she continued, "It is kind of amazing that they let go of the entire accounting department. I would have thought your old group was the one they would definitely want to have around, since you all dealt with money."

"You would think, but I guess that is the future. New technology allows them to do with one or two people what took a whole team in the past. I guess it is just what it will be; technology is going to replace all of us, and there isn't a damn thing we can do about it." Jamal jammed another fork full of chicken and rice into his mouth as his eyes shifted away from Marguerite and down to the plate, now half full of food. As he chewed, his thoughts returned to the email and what would happen next. Marguerite sat staring at Jamal. She was taken aback by his negative demeanor and sullen attitude, something which she could not recall ever having seen during their prior years together. When describing him, she believed that "calm" and "nonchalant" were understatements for a man she found unflappable, almost to a fault. A part of her felt that his lack of emotional responses —at least visible ones—gave him an advantage in their relationship, as she wore her emotions on her sleeve for the whole world to see. She opened her mouth slightly to speak, but decided against it, opting instead to continue eating in silence.

BREAKING NEWS

Jamal sat in the small white room he had turned into a home office. It had been eight days since he sent the email, and during that time the responses from most of the parties blind carbon copied on it slowly started to fill up his inbox. The bulk of the responses followed the same format: "Thank you for the email. We reviewed your submission and decided not to pursue your submission any further. Thank you again and we look forward to future submissions." Generic responses which made him believe they had not even read his message. Other responses questioned the validity of his information, and a couple even accused him of disinformation, stopping just short of saying he lied. But eventually he did receive three responses which indicated an interest in his story, which led to further emails, then phone calls, and eventually the publication of the contents of his email on the front page of a national newspaper. Within hours of the publication, most of the national news channels were reporting on it. After that, and despite having an unlisted number, Jamal's phone constantly rang with people requesting interviews. He hoped for some interest in the information he shared, but in no way expected nor was he prepared for the level of interest it was garnering.

After nearly two straight days of phone calls and emails, he began to shut down mentally and emotionally, retreating to the little office in the middle of the night, leaving Marguerite to sleep alone in their queen bed. In the morning, Marguerite loudly called out for Jamal from their bedroom and then the kitchen—acts he found unnecessary since there weren't many places for him to be in their small apartment. When she entered the office a few moments later, she chided him for not responding and asked what he was doing in the office. Apologizing for not answering, Jamal said he was checking emails. A sigh of frustration escaped as she gazed upon him, staring at the computer and unfazed by her noticeable irritation with him, she commented on the time and that he was still wearing pajamas.

At that moment, Jamal debated whether he should finally tell her the truth. He had initially acted out of impulse—something completely unusual for him—which is why he had not disclosed to her on that fateful night. But since that night, he had continued to keep everything a secret, both because he was uncertain what would happen after he sent the email, and what her reaction would be. However, he was confident one of her emotional responses would be anger with him for acting without telling her first. He knew the truth would come out sooner or later, but apparently, she had not read or even noticed the news story. This was not surprising to him, since most of her time was spent working at the clinic, typing patient notes at home, and watching baking shows before drifting off to sleep.

Further, the topic of business was never her sort of thing, so even if she did look at the news, it was unlikely she would even have paid attention to the news story. In the end, he decided against the truth, instead opting to tell her he was going to change in a moment, once he finished some work—both lies, but she did not seem to notice. Marguerite took a few steps forward, said she needed to leave, and they exchanged a brief kiss before she turned and walked out of the room. Jamal watched her leave before turning his attention back to the blue monitor screen and clicking on the email icon.

'Knock...knock, knock, knock...knock!'

Jamal glanced at the clock on the computer screen: 2:38 PM. He shifted his gaze from the monitor toward the office door as suddenly he felt stirrings of fear. A second time the sound of four repetitive thuds against the front door echoed throughout the apartment. Jamal felt the onset of a sudden panic.

"Hello, Jamal al-Bashir," a male voice with a distinctly southern accent shouted from the other side of the front door. Jamal remained glued to the chair, overcome with a sense of dread at what was to come next. "Mr. al-Bashir are you in there?" the voice continued. Jamal stood up from his chair and tiptoed cautiously from his office to the hallway. Before reaching the front door, he abruptly stopped. He considered remaining silent and retreating into the office, in hopes that who ever it was may go away, but his curiosity won out in the end.

"Who is it?" he asked, standing about two feet from the door.

"It's CMPD, the police," the male voice responded. "We would like to talk with you Mr. al-Bashir, if you would please open the door."

"I don't want to talk with you," Jamal hastily replied.

"Jamal, would you please come to the door so we may speak?"

"No, as I said, I don't want to talk."

"Jamal, please come to the door," the voice trailed off as a moment of silence filled the air.

"Look Jamal, we have a warrant for your arrest," another, deeper male voice with a non-descript accent shouted through the door. "You can either come to the door or we can do this the hard way. Trust me, you don't want to do it the hard way."

Recoiling, Jamal, rushed in panic back to the office. His first thought was to close and barricade the office door, but he decided against it, and instead ran over to his desk. As he stood, looking over the desk, the black metallic object caught his attention.

"I, I..." he started to say before realizing he was speaking too softly for anyone to hear. Shaking, he picked up the gun. "I HAVE A GUN!" Jamal heard the deep voice shout "He has a gun" and then two other voices which were further away repeated the same warning. Gaining some control of his nerves, Jamal reached down with his still-shaking hand and picked up the gun, feeling the cool, smooth metal of the barrel in his left hand as his right grasped the handle.

"Jamal, Jamal, please don't do anything stupid," the first male voice shouted.

"I HAVE A GUN!" Jamal screamed before pausing to look around the room. Through the window, he could see the flashing blue lights creeping in through the half-closed blinds. "Please, please, just leave me alone," he begged.

"I'm afraid we can't do that Jamal," replied the first male voice. "Look, Jamal, please just put down the gun and come to the front door. It will be a lot better for all of us if you put down the gun and come talk to us."

"I'm afraid I can't do that," Jamal responded, his shaking arm moving to point the gun toward the office door, and then he turned it on himself.

THE NOTE

I hope you never need to go any further than this page.
I wrote the enclosed letter because, in case anything
should happen to me, I want the world to know what
happened. There is a lot I still don't know myself, but I
am hoping with time and more investigation I can figure
out what is really going on and report on it. However, in
the unfortunate event that something should happen to
me, then I'm asking you to bring to light what I have
discovered. In that event, my wish is that you make
public in its entirety the contents of the aforementioned
letter. I know it is a bit lengthy, but I think it is
important to know the full details, so that there are no
questions about what I found and how I found it. I'm
guessing that, based off this cryptic message, you may
want to read the letter.

But I implore you, please don't read the enclosed
letter unless you find out I'm dead or you learn that
some other serious event has happened to me. In that
event, then please do everything in your power to get
the contents of the letter and the information in the
enclosed thumb drive released to the public. The public
needs to know, or else all of this, everything I've given
up, has been for nothing.

BACKGROUND

*I'm an auditor. Probably not the most intriguing, inter*esting, or glamorous job out there. And definitely not the first thing you want to tell someone when they ask what you do. It is not as impressive sounding as "I'm a doctor" or as cool as saying "I'm a pilot". It does not conjure up emotions of gratitude and reverence like saying "I'm a soldier" or "I'm a firefighter" or any number of other jobs out there. "I'm an auditor" is not a conversation starter at parties and at work it seems to be a great way to kill any conversation. In fact, most employees probably see auditors like me as the enemy, someone coming in to judge their work, to find problems, and then to formally write them up in some report no one really wants to read. That is why they probably avoid talking to auditors. And I can't blame them. I never thought I would be an auditor. No, instead I thought I would be CEO of some cutting-edge startup, but ten years after finishing my MBA, I found myself working as an auditor. Well, technically my title is principal audit leader, which is as ridiculous as it sounds, working at South Lake Union Management Corporation, although South Lake is how everybody refers to it for short. Probably never heard of it before now; well neither had I until about two years ago when a recruiter contacted me out of the blue and said they were hiring.

Now, while you might never have heard of South Lake Union Management Corporation, you definitely have heard of Peaked, Inc., the behemoth online retailer. An amazing company in a way. It was started in the mid-1990's by two friends in Colorado who created an online discussion board—Peaked Interest, a play on words in-corporating the nearby Pike's Peak—to talk about classic 1980 movies and video games. This then evolved within a couple years to them selling these retro items that they found through discussions with other members and at random comic book and video game conventions. Within five years, this little on-the-side retail company had ballooned into selling virtually everything else, from books and comic books to blenders and coffee makers. As business exploded, Peaked Interest was shortened to "Peaked"— a sort of cheeky attempt at irony as the business had anything but peaked. The logo remained a silhouette of that famous Colorado mountain.

Now, like many Fortune 500 companies, Peaked has multiple revenue streams, as well as massive earnings on par with, if not exceeding, the GDP of some small nations, all of which it needs to manage. And this is where South Lake comes into play. South Lake is the company that manages all of the accounts receivable for Peaked, as well as for Peaked's more than 100 different affiliates and subsidiaries scattered across the globe.

South Lake processes incoming payments, executes transactions with vendors, handles collecting on debts owed, and a variety of other functions too numerous to mention here. But unlike Peaked, with its thousands of employees and hundreds of locations, South Lake is small—with around two hundred employees, of which twelve work in the audit department, all located in one location—Charlotte, North Carolina, far removed from Peaked's dual corporate headquarters.

My job within this little audit department is performing the Anti-Money Laundering ("AML") audits for the company. Sounds neat and quite important, right, working to prevent terrorists, drug lords, and the mafia from laundering their money? Sadly, it is not what most people think. Rather than the Jack Ryan, James Bond, or other secret agent lifestyle of traveling the world, sneaking about in dark alleys or getting in car chases, that people may picture; most of what I do is read policies and procedures, ask questions, write memos, and occasionally look at Excel files full of transactions. As for the travel, I have gotten to do a bit of it, but instead of exciting locations like Istanbul, Monaco, or Tokyo, my travel has often been repeated trips to places like Detroit or Minneapolis, and as of late mainly Colorado Springs, Colorado, and Boston, Massachusetts, the respective West and East Coast head-quarters of Peaked.

Other aspects of the job were on par with what you probably would think of a typical corporate job. The pay is okay, not great, not nearly what others in the industry earn, especially those who work for tech giants like Google or insurance companies, but it could be worse, and it works for me being single, without a family to support. I have been doing AML work for nearly a decade with little excitement or stories to show for it. Perhaps the only interesting thing to happen to me during this time was finding a payment that was almost made to a corrupt Venezuelan politician. But even this event was not that exciting, as I had little to do with it since the payment was canceled at the last minute by an alert employee before I even spotted it. Contrary to what most people might think, this was a rather mundane job, at least that was until three weeks ago when I learned about Account 44-56-7289-01.

ACCOUNT 44-56-7289-01

It started on October 3rd, when on that day the U.S. Attorney's Office for the District of Colorado announced they were indicting one senior executive and two mid-level employees at Peaked. Who the accused were is not important; however, what they were accused of—embezzlement, wire fraud, and conspiracy to commit wire fraud—is what matters. The story made news across the country, from the front page of The Wall Street Journal to the lead headline of The Denver Post as well as most of the local Charlotte news outlets. I was running on the treadmill at the gym after work when I saw the story come up on the six o'clock news. There were not many details at that time but what was reported was essentially that a senior executive devised a plan to embezzle hundreds of thousands from Peaked. This executive enlisted the help of two mid-level employees who oversaw payments made to vendors. These two employees used their access to di-vert portions of payments from legitimate vendors to an account they had established for themselves. Within minutes of the news story ending, my phone vibrated, and I saw my boss's name, Jayson Hart, appear on the screen. I stopped the treadmill and read the message: "U probably saw the news, see you in my of-fice in the morning. Get there early."

The next morning, I arrived at work at 6:45 am, a whole hour-and-a-half before I typically came into the of-fice. When I arrived outside Jayson's office, I saw through his glass door that there were two other people there with him. I immediately recognized the stocky, redheaded woman in her late forties wearing a green dress emblazoned with some kind of hideous print as Susan Henderson, Head of Human Resources for South Lake. The other person, a tall, thin, balding man in his mid-to-late-sixties, whom I had never seen before, stood near her, and in sharp contrast, wore a slim fit, perfectly tailored, navy blue suit.

As I stood looking through the glass, I saw Jayson hold up his hand like a stop sign, indicating that I was to remain outside the office. I took a seat in a chair in an empty cubicle near the office and for the first time began to wonder what the meeting was about. My mind started racing, trying to come up with a plausible reason why Jayson would be meeting with the Head of HR before meeting with me. Was I somehow connected to the criminal case from the news? Had I missed something during one of my audits and were they now going to fire me? I could feel sweat collecting in my armpits and pooling in my lower back as I stared at Jayson's door. I was formulating excuses—I'm just one person, we don't have the resources, I can't test everything—when Jayson's door opened and the three occupants exited.

Susan and the tall man continued walking toward the elevators while Jayson motioned for me to come in as he went back into his office. I stood up gingerly, as my legs were still shaking and I felt lightheaded, but managed to walk over and into Jayson's office, trying to conceal the sweat stains that had formed on my light blue button-up shirt.

"Well, looks like you are about to be busy," Jayson said as I entered the office. Jayson was wearing a tight black polo shirt which seemed to be one size too small. Like many bodybuilders, Jayson enjoyed showing off his muscles, even in the workplace, not realizing that those around him joked behind his back about his tight clothes. Matching his wardrobe were his closely cropped hair and reddish tan, all of which screamed "look at me, I'm a bodybuilder," yet at the same time his appearance was bland, almost entirely non-descript and unnoteworthy, much like his personality. As I walked over to the two seats in front of his desk, he said, with no need, except to reinforce his status as my manager, "Please, take a seat."

"Good morning," I said, trying to calm my nerves as I sat down in the seat.

"Oh, yes, good morning, sorry, it has been quite a day and it's not even, what, seven-thirty," Jayson responded looking down at his smart watch. "Anyway, thank you for coming in early this morning."

"Sure, no problem," I replied, trying to sound upbeat to hide the anxiety in my voice. I looked around his office hoping to take my mind off why I might be there. The walls of the office were painted a generic cream color.

Both the left and right walls were completely bare and the wall behind him would have been the same, except for a large whiteboard which took up the middle of the wall. There were a few notes scribbled on the whiteboard pertaining to the audit schedule, but what struck me for the first time was how devoid his office was of personal artifacts. There were no pictures, no trophies, no kitschy travel items, nothing that made that office any different than any number of the other offices located in the building. This really should have come as no surprise. While I had never pictured myself being an auditor, once I was one, I fully embraced it, with career aspirations to someday be a Chief Audit Officer or Audit Director at a major company like Ford, BlackRock, GE or 3M. Jayson, however, never fully bought into the role of audit. He had previously been on the business side at some major tech companies in the Bay Area, but after being laid off twice in one year, decided to move east and accepted his current role with South Lake. It was obvious to anyone who knew him even slightly, that this role was nothing more than a stopgap before moving back into a business role.

"So yes, the reason you are here," Jayson started, lowering his head in thought as he used both arms to shift his body in his seat. "You no doubt saw the news yesterday, about the Peaked employees who were indicted on embezzlement and fraud charges."

"Yes, I saw the news right before you texted me."

"Right, well good, actually not good, but you know what I mean. Anyway, as you probably can guess, a lot of people around Peaked and around here are asking a bunch of questions. The typical 'how long did this happen' and 'was anyone else involved' as well as other questions. We know the answer, for the most part to one of those questions, but not the other."

"Okay," I said after a brief pause.

In that moment, Jayson seemed lost in thought. I was looking at him as he turned his face away from his computer monitor and toward the notepad on his desk. His eyes rapidly dashed from left to right, as though he were quickly reading whatever was written on the little yellowish pad of paper.

"So, before I forget and go any further, anything we discuss in here must remain in here. It can't be discussed with others unless I tell you it is okay to, you understand right, nothing new, you know the drill about not discussing our work?"

"Yes, yes I do," I replied as my anxiety began to vanish upon realizing that this conversation was not leading to a statement that I was fired.

"Okay, good. So, as I was saying, we, I mean those with a need to know, have learned from the Feds that their investigation showed the embezzlement had been going on for the past eighteen months. Now that isn't to say it wasn't going on longer, but since the Feds apparently were investigating this case for a while, there seems to be little reason to doubt them."

"That makes sense," I said in agreement. I had an idea from years of doing this work, attending industry conventions and reading the news, that the Justice Department didn't typically bring charges without having most, if not all, of the evidence they needed.

"But what the Feds can't tell us for sure, and what everyone around here wants to know, is if anyone else was involved or worse yet, if anyone else is doing something similar right now. And that apparently is what has the Board upset. They want to know if this was an isolated situation or if there is a bigger problem. And that is where you fit in. I have a 'special assignment' which you are to begin looking into immediately," Jayson said using his pointer and index fingers to make air quotes as he said special assignment.

"Immediately?" I asked.

"Yes, like once you leave this office, you need to start working on this."

"But what about my audit that just kicked off?"

"Don't worry about it right now, just focus on this assignment and when you finish go back to the audit," he replied and then paused, looking at me, seemingly trying to gauge my reaction. "I've also been given authority to hire an external firm who could work on any of your audits, in case you find something during this special assignment and need more time."

"Okay, but if you've been given authority to hire an external firm to do my job, couldn't you hire them instead to look into this? I mean doesn't it make sense to go out and hire someone with experience in doing forensic accounting and finding embezzlement?"

"Maybe, but this needs to remain in-house. Orders from the top. Senior management wants to know if there is a bigger issue here before they go back to the Board and make the very public move of hiring an external firm. Does that make sense?"

"I understand that, but I wouldn't even know where to begin, that is why an external firm that specializes in this stuff would be much better; they know where to start and more importantly what to look for," I said, pleading my case.

"Oh now, I'm sure you can do it just as well as someone from outside. That is why we hired you, because you have experience in this. I mean, isn't money laundering the same as embezzlement," he asked with a smirk as he knew I really only had one way of answering his question.

"Not really, the two are not the same, and I don't know how I would even start a project like this," I replied, knowing the response was not the one he anticipated and could backfire on me.

"Oh, well I'm sure you will be able to figure it out," he responded as the smile disappeared from his face. I could tell he was becoming agitated. This was clearly not an assignment open for debate, let alone discussion, and I figured it was best to just get out of there while I still had a job.

"Okay, I'll get to it."

"Oh, and if you do find something, bring it back to me, don't tell anyone else, just come right to me," Jayson said as I stood up and began walking out of the office.

"Will do," I said without stopping as I exited the room.

"What the hell have I gotten myself into," I thought

as I walked back to my cubicle and powered up my laptop. As I entered my login information, my mind began racing again trying to solve the problem I kept asking myself since Jayson's office – "How do I even start this?" Contrary to what Jayson said, this was not the same as the work to which I had become accustomed. With money laundering, essentially 'dirty' money (funds tied to a criminal activity) is put into one account and then moved around to other accounts or businesses, so that the funds at the end are 'clean', meaning they no longer can be tied back to the original funds.

Embezzlement, however, is something different, as the money is already 'clean' but the funds are diverted from an intended account into another account, typically a personal account the embezzler can access. Unlike money-laundering, where you are looking at the source of the money coming in – the individuals contributing the initial funds, their source of income, where the money is coming from, and so on – with embezzlement, the money is in the company, but someone is doing something to siphon some of it away from a legitimate cause into their own account. I had the tools, experience, and knowledge to find those suspicious external accounts and customers worth investigating for money laundering. There were always clues, little nuggets of information, which gave away the activity, and I knew how to sift through the data to find them. With embezzlement, to say I was at a loss other than knowing what it was, would completely be an understatement.

I stared at my screen for probably the better part of

an hour, if not much longer. I am a bit ashamed to admit that during this time, I did an occasional internet search for key words like 'embezzlement' and 'catching embezzlers', but to no avail. It was after nine o'clock, and I could feel the early morning wake-up catching up with me, so I decided to grab a coffee as I was getting nowhere fast sitting there. After a walk to the brightly lit breakroom, I stood in front of the little black machine brewing my single cup of coffee, and it struck me. Rather than looking for suspicious accounts or money movements, like I was used to doing, I should look at the money going out. I rushed back to my desk before my coffee was even finished, as I did not want to lose the idea while waiting for some cheap coffee.

Back at my desk, I accessed Peaked's payment system, MoneyBridge, which essentially kept a ledger of almost all of the funds received and disbursed outside of wages and some other minor revenue streams. Unlike the rest of the audit department, I had access to this, as well as a number of other key Peaked systems, because I occasion-ally had to test the systems and investigate suspicious ac-tivities. I figured that if there was anyone else embezzling money, they would be doing so via MoneyBridge and not payroll. I knew that HR and the payroll departments monitored wages like hawks, having experienced their diligence myself.

Once I received a couple hundred more dollars in my paycheck than I should have due to a timing issue with my bonus, and within two days of the funds being deposited in my bank account, I received three phone calls, half-a-dozen emails, not including those sent to Jayson, regarding this overpayment and the funds were clawed back. Perhaps payroll and HR's excessive monitoring was due to the outdated system they used for wages, or because that would be the first place an employee would try to steal funds. Either way, I felt confident that if someone did try to embezzle through the payroll system, they would have been caught within days of their first attempt. But MoneyBridge was different—it was simpler. Money received from sales was run through specific algorithms which split the proceeds up amongst the external parties (e.g., vendors, content creators, authors, etc.) and Peaked based on pre-set revenue shares per product category. Since it was a newer system and relied on preset payment distributions, there were fewer people monitoring it on a daily basis.

Doing a simple query of the prior month's data, I quickly realized the enormity of the task in front of me. There were over 80,000 transactions in the prior month, nearly 3,000 a day, to over 10,000 different accounts. My head lightly hit my desk when I saw the number of transactions, way more than I anticipated and could even wrap my head around at the moment. The embezzler or team of them could be fleecing the company and their activity would easily be hidden in the sheer volume of transactions. I felt like I was at a loss again, but before panicking, decided to export the data and run it up against some of the algorithms I had to catch suspicious accounts.

Unfortunately, either because of the sheer number of transactions or because my algorithms weren't designed for this type of review, I was having no luck. Each query I ran resulted in at best nearly one-third of the transactions being flagged as suspicious or more often in the program crashing, leaving me to start over again. I must have tried over one hundred different attempts, skipping lunch in the process, with nothing to show for it. With the time nearing four o'clock, I sat back in my seat and closed my eyes. My thoughts focused on the lack of progress I had made, and I began to worry my new task was impossible for me to accomplish. In ten years of working, I had never failed to do something I was assigned, but was beginning to panic that this assignment, with all the attention it had from the Board and senior management, would be my first failure, a spectacular one at that, and the timing itself could not be worse.

I took a couple deep breaths, trying to calm myself and looked back at my monitors, full of line after line of numbers. The screens looked blurry and I could feel how tired my eyes had become. As I rubbed both eyes with the palms of my hands, I decided to try scanning through the data manually. Thirty minutes later, I still was not seeing anything that on the face of it looked to be suspicious. There were no odd payments or payments that did not match the classification code. However, as I sifted through the data, one account – Account 44-56-7289-01 – kept reappearing. This was not unusual, as there were plenty of accounts which were listed over and over; however, what made this one unique compared to the others were the first four numbers. Most often the accounts I reviewed have the same first numbers, with only the trailing numbers being different for each account. Looking at the data, I could see this pattern playing out with numerous different accounts having the same first few numbers, indicating these accounts were all with the same institution. This was true for all the accounts listed except for Account 44-56-7289-01, which was the only one beginning with 44-56. With nothing else to go on, I figured this would be my best and only place to start my investigation.

I plugged 44-56-7289-01 into MoneyBridge and searched for all payments made over the prior twelve months. After the data loaded, I quickly realized that I probably was on to something. For the first month there were a handful of transactions involving the account; however, in each subsequent month thereafter the transactions grew exponentially. Now this alone was not entirely unusual, as new sellers on Peaked often grew their sales steadily over time as they learned how to market their products, advertise, and take advantage of word-of-mouth or social media promotion. However, what made the growth of the transactions for Account 44-56-7289-01 different from those I had seen was just how quickly it was growing. Twelve months ago, less than $250 was deposited in the account; however, this amount more than doubled each month thereafter, so that in September, twelve months later, nearly $700,000 was deposited. It was the type of growth that would make even the best start-up or Fortune 500 company envious. Growth that seemed unnatural, and for good reason, because it was.

After a whole day of searching and hitting nothing but dead ends, I finally felt like I had made some progress.

But I knew I needed to know much more, particularly who owned the account and where it was located. I could not see this information in MoneyBridge and would require access to payment systems I did not have access to, but I knew who would. Alex Bashir was a senior tax manager in the accounting department. While his title was perhaps better than auditor, I felt like what he did was even less appealing. He and his team handled the tax matters related to all of the independent sellers, other than national retailers, who sold anything on Peaked. I looked at the clock in the lower right-hand corner of my computer screen and saw it was ten minutes to five. "Shoot, he's likely gone for the day" I thought. Forgetting Jayson's warning not to discuss the matter with anyone, I typed up a brief email asking Alex to look into Account 44-56-7289-01 and let me know to whom it belonged, where they were located, how long it had been opened, and if there was anything unusual about it. I then closed my laptop, left work, and went to the gym to clear my head.

The next day, I arrived at work at 9:15 am, much later than usual, as I decided to sleep in that morning after a restless night. Despite being tired, I had spent the previous night running through in my mind possible scenarios for embezzling money. After opening my email, I saw, tucked in the middle of the dozen or so messages, that I had received a response from Alex at 8:57 that morning. I opened the message which read:

This account is one of ours. See below:

Account No.: 44-56-7289-01

Account Name: Peaked Corp. R&D GAIGE

Account Owner: Peaked USA, Inc.

Opened: 2022

Location: 5153 SE Tremont Ave, Denver, CO 80202, USA

Description: Internal account – Tax Treatment N/A

Alexander al-Bashir

Finance Manager, Tax Reporting

South Lake Union Management Corporation

Even though Alex's email was short, I re-read it at least two more times. I could not make sense of it. Why was an internal account receiving third party payments? And what was this account? I figured the "R&D" meant Research and Development, but I had no idea why this department would be receiving payments from customers. What were they selling, and why were they being treated the same as vendors? I knew Peaked already had a division which sold directly to customers. However, the payments to this division were coded differently in MoneyBridge and all payments were deposited into one specific account, which was not this one. So why were these internal R&D payments showing up in the same transaction history as payments to *Joe's Handmade Wood Toys* and *The LowCountry Bookstore*? My mind was filled with questions for which I did not have any answers, but I felt like I was on the right track. I did not have enough information to go back to Jayson— at least I felt I did not— but I was much more confident I was searching in the right place compared to twenty-four hours prior.

THE CALL THAT STARTED IT ALL

I spent the rest of the morning split between working on the audit I had started just days before and thinking over what I needed to do next with my "special assignment". Like a daily ritual, around noon most of the people in the office began to leave to get food from one of the restaurants which lined the streets outside our office. I was staring blankly at my screen, my mind lost in thought about how to proceed when, for some reason I can't explain, my train of thought was interrupted by a glimpse of orange to my left. I turned completely around in my swivel chair to look and caught a glimpse of Paige Caruso, in a bright orange blouse walking past my desk with Hersh Patel. Paige was a compliance officer who covered the technology group for South Lake. As I watched her walk away, it occurred to me she might have connections who could help get me in contact with the R&D department. I quickly jumped from my seat and rushed over to her.

"Hey Paige, Paige, I was wondering if you might have a moment," I said, stopping about two feet away from her and Hersh. Both of them turned to look at me as we stood in the middle of the large, open space between the cubicles where my desk was located, and the elevator banks where they were headed.

"Hey, yes sure, we were about to go get lunch though," she said, facing me.

"No problem, this will be quick," I said reassuringly. "And if it is okay, can this just be you and me? Sorry Hersh."

"Umm, okay, I hope I'm not being audited," Paige chuckled nervously, as she gave a little nod to Hersh, who then walked a few feet away. "So, what's up—why do you need to talk to me in private?"

"Yes, well, I'm working on something at the moment which might involve the R&D department over at Peaked. Anyway, I was wondering if you might know someone in that department or someone in our IT department who might be able to get me in contact with a person in the R&D department at Peaked? I've never had to deal with them and am afraid I wouldn't know where to start, so I was hoping for your help."

"Huh, hmmm, well you could probably reach out to Nick Stern. He's in the business programs team at Peaked covering new products, so he might be able to give you someone to contact in R&D."

"Awesome, Nick Stern, spelled like S-T-E-R-N?" I asked.

"Yes, that's it," Paige responded as a look of puzzle-ment crossed her face. "What's this about anyway; why do you need to talk to someone in R&D at Peaked?"

"Well, it's part of an audit that...," I began to reply before pausing as I recalled Jayson's admonition. "Sorry, I can't say more, not that I don't trust you, but you know, we can't discuss pending audits. Anyway, thanks for the contact, and sorry I can't say more, but I know you need to get to lunch, and I have, ahh, a meeting, so yes, thanks again."

Before Paige could say anything more, I turned and walked briskly back to my desk. As I sat down, I turned to look back where we had been standing, but the space was empty, as Paige and Hersh must have continued on to the elevators. I replayed the conversation over in my head, not just the bit about Nick Stern, but the whole thing. I cringed at the thought of how awkward the conversation had been, and wanted to put it all behind me. As my feelings of anxiety began to subside, I logged into my computer, went to the Peaked global directory, and searched for Nick Stern.

Two results appeared, one for Nicholas A. Stern, whose job title was business execution officer and another for Jonathan Nicholas Stern, whose job title was lead systems engineer. I had no idea what either person's job title meant, and knowing Peaked, neither did they, but I felt Jonathan Nicholas was who I needed, as his job title seemed the most "IT" like, even despite the fact his first name was not actually Nick. I typed up a brief email to Jonathan Nicholas, introducing myself and asking him if he was familiar with the Peaked research and development department. I included the account name – Peaked Corp. R&D GAIGE – to add greater specificity and then hit send. After a quick check of the news and sports, I was about to log off for lunch, when a notification popped up in the lower right-hand corner of the screen indicating a new email. Checking the inbox, I noticed Nick had responded.

Call me in 5 min, at my **cell** – 704-555-2638, **not the office** line.
Nick
J. Nicholas Stern
AVP, Business Initiative & Data Analytics

"Wow, the guy's quick," I thought to myself. I was beginning to feel myself fade, as I was intermittent fasting, meaning no food between 8:00 pm and noon, and desperately wanted to go grab something to eat. I wasn't big on diets, but after my ex-girlfriend left me, with a comment about being fat, I could not shake the feeling I needed to lose weight, and had heard good things about intermittent fasting. But before leaving for lunch, I could tell from Nick's email, which was unusually brief and oddly bolded, even for Peaked employees, that lunch needed to wait until after calling him. The next five minutes felt like an hour as I tried suppressing my hunger while also wondering why he made a point about calling his cell. At 12:24, I picked up my cell phone, as something told me I should use my personal rather than office phone, and dialed 555-2638.

"Hi, Nick, this is—" I started when I heard the click on the other end of the line indicating someone had picked up.

"Yeah, yeah, yeah, hey are you calling from the office

line or something else," Nick asked, abruptly interrupting me.

"I'm calling from my personal phone," I replied.

"Good, good," Nick responded, before taking a brief pause. "Okay, so look, I don't have a lot of time, but you had a question about R&D."

"Yes, well, um, yeah, um," I was caught off guard by Nick's abruptness and struggled to find my words for a moment. "Well, um, uh, I'm working on something at the moment, can't really get too much into what it is, but, yes, I wanted to talk to someone with the R&D department."

"Alright, and these questions of yours are about GAIGE," he asked and before I could respond continued. "Your email mentioned GAIGE, so I assumed that is what you wanted to talk about, right?"

"I mean, possibly," I started as I frantically scrolled through my email and re-read my message to Nick. "Yes, I am curious about an R&D account, which I guess has Gaige in it, is that how you say it, Gaige?"

"Yes, that's right, Gaige, like in a car," Nick responded. "So, what do you want to know?"

"Well, I guess I'm curious about, um, really I'm trying to understand some payments being made into the R&D account," I replied. There was a brief pause, and from my interaction thus far, I could tell he probably wanted more information. But in that split second break, I remembered that I wasn't supposed to be talking to anyone about this. I knew I could not tell him why I was looking into this account, but I needed to tell him something.

"See, I'm in the audit department at South Lake, primarily covering AML, anti-money laundering, and part of my work involves confirming money moving from one account to another is appropriate; usual audit stuff, you know. And look, I'm not saying there is anything suspicious with this account, I just need to double check, do my due diligence, you know."

"Oh, so you don't know what it is," he asked, and then, after a brief pause, correctly assumed that I did not. "Alright, I guess you would want to talk with Javed Ag..., Aga.., Agawall, it's something like that. His first name is definitely Javed, should be easy to find. He's in charge of GAIGE now, I believe".

"Okay, great– thank you," I said, but as I was about to end the call, one question crept in my mind; something I would have been better off never asking, but did. "Wait, I do have one question, if you don't mind?"

"Sure, what is it," Nick responded impatiently.

"Well, your email was a bit odd. You highlighted you wanted me to call your cell phone, and then when I called, you asked if I was calling from the office phone, like it was bad or something if I did."

"Okay, and your point?," he shot back.

"Um, well, it was odd," I replied. "Why were you so concerned with us not talking on the office lines. What is there that I'm missing or need to know?"

"You're looking into payments going into the R&D GAIGE account, right?," he asked, which I confirmed I was. "Well, you are right, there is something there, something suspicious."

"Really, what is it, is someone embezz..., um, is someone stealing money?," I asked, kicking myself for saying too much and knowing Nick probably knew exactly what I was doing and looking for at the moment.

"No, not stealing, at least in the way you might be thinking about it, but much worse. It is much...," and then he paused a couple seconds before continuing. "Look, I've said enough, I really actually need to go. I've got a meeting in like – well, now – but talk to Javed and you'll see."

"Okay, but it seems like you know something, maybe something I should know before I talk to anyone else," I pressed. I heard Nick exhale loudly on the other end of the line.

"Um, okay, you want something, I'll give you one name – A.W. Bucher – find him and you will begin to understand," Nick said. "Anyway, as I said, I really do have to go, I've got a meeting now. Bye."

The line then went dead. It was 12:30 pm, and my stomach was turning over on itself from hunger, which only got worse during the call. But before I set off to grab some food, I entered the name A.W. Bucher into the employee directory, with no hits. I then searched for the name on the internet. The first item in the search results was for a book titled *The Weeping Moon* written by an A.W. Bucher that linked back to the Peaked website. Of course, the book was for sale on Peaked, no surprise there. The next result was for a Swiss parts company and then the third result was again for the book *The Weeping Moon*, although this time the link was to a small secondhand bookstore. I scrolled through the next fifteen or so results, but aside from the first and third results, none of the other results was a close, let alone direct, match to A.W. Bucher. "Maybe I entered the name wrong" I thought to myself.

A nagging feeling swept over me that the info I needed was right in front of me, but somehow, I was missing it. Since the first hit for A.W. Bucher happened to be a link to Peaked's bookstore website, I decided that would be the best place to look. The page for A.W. Bucher's *The Weeping Moon* looked the same as any other book page on Peaked. There was a picture of the book cover, a pop-art style picture of a silver moon set against a dark blue background with tears falling into a glistening silver pond below the moon and the title written in bold yellow letters. The book had a 7.9 out of 10 rating, so I clicked on the "reviews" tab at the top of the screen to see what people had to say about the book.

The first five, and most recent, reviews offered up the same general description – readable, but unimaginative, predictable plot and poorly developed characters. Scrolling down through the latest ten or so reviews, I noticed all were in the range of 4, 5, or 6, with nothing above a 7. "How the hell can this thing have a 7.9 rating?" I muttered as I scrolled down to the bottom of the page and clicked on the blue number "2" icon which instantly moved to the next page of reviews. I noticed all of the reviews on this page offered much more favorable, albeit briefer summaries of the book, with each rating an 8 or above. As I examined the reviews in more detail, I noticed they all were written more than six months ago, while the less positive reviews on the first page were written within the past three months.

It seemed odd, the dichotomy of the older versus newer reviews. But part of me wondered if the reviewers were just copying each other, not wanting to not be part of the bandwagon. I felt like I had seen that with movie reviews recently, so perhaps the same mentality applied to book reviews. Moving back to the main page for the book, I read the author's bio to see if there was anything there. Unfortunately, A.W. Bucher's minibiography was about as generic as one would expect for a writer. He had attended Georgetown University, graduating with a degree in journalism, and worked for the Washington Post and Baltimore Sun, where he covered local crime for over a decade before finally deciding to write his first novel, which was loosely based off his time covering gangs in west Baltimore. Even his picture was rather generic—a middle-aged white man, with closely trimmed red hair, standing arms crossed in front of a bookshelf full of books. Perhaps the only unique thing in his photo were the large, thick half-rimmed black glasses he wore, and even that wasn't too memorable. Sitting there, staring at the screen, feeling as though I was no closer to knowing anything than before, I decided it was time to grab lunch. I locked my computer screen and walked down the stairs located near the elevator bank to Rhino Shoppe.

Sitting at the counter eating my spicy Italian half-sub sandwich, I repeatedly played the entire conversation over in my head. The first time was to make sure I remembered everything. The second time was to see if there was something I missed— some word or statement that might shed light on the investigation. The third and final time was not due to doubts in my memory but to analyze Nick's behavior. I could not help but think there was something odd about the way Nick had acted. In fact, I knew there was something odd. But even more, it was clear there was something Nick had wanted to say, some secret or the sort, but he felt he could not. As the conversation replayed in my mind for that final time, I became confident that this hunch was correct. There was something Nick was hiding, some secret he wanted to tell but that he did not feel comfortable saying to a stranger, especially one from Audit no doubt. "What kind of secret could it be?" I wondered.

After a quick lunch, I returned to my desk and searched the Peaked employee directory for Javed. The search returned thirteen Javeds, seven of whom whose last name started with an 'A', and of those, five worked in the Technology department. Without more details, I felt lost, a feeling that was becoming all too common, yet no less disagreeable. I knew I couldn't contact all five of them to see who the correct person was, because to do so would risk word of my investigation spreading even more. If Jayson learned from someone else that I was asking around, without telling him first, I probably would find myself reprimanded, or even fired.

No, I needed to narrow the list down as much as possible. Luckily, when searching each Javed on the internet, I noticed that one of them, a Javed Agarwal, had listed GAIGE on his LinkedIn profile. I immediately shot him an email asking if he might have time to talk about GAIGE. I then sat at my desk, staring at my email inbox, waiting for a response, but after ten minutes, with no response, I decided to go back to working on the audit I had started. I figured it was best to not think about R&D, GAIGE, and embezzlement anymore, before it consumed even more of my time and life than it already had.

MACHINE LEARNING

*The next couple of days went by as normally as any be-*fore I had been given the special assignment. I had my initial calls with the business I was auditing, reviewed documents, and began planning the scope of my audit. Work was once again familiar to me, with nothing that caused me much mental stress, and I was even beginning to forget about the embezzlement assignment, account 44-56-7289-01, R&D, and Nick Stern. My memory of the prior week faded rapidly over the week, so much so that when a pleasantly sunny and cool Saturday and Sunday arrived, I took part in morning tennis matches followed by afternoons spent at Olde Meck and NODA breweries, without a single thought about the assignment.

On Tuesday morning of the following week, I had completely removed all thoughts about the "special as-signment" by the time I had my bi-weekly 10:00 am meeting with Jayson. The meeting started out as nor-mally as ever, chatting about what was going on in each other's lives, discussing fantasy football, and debating which college football team looked like they were the best. I still maintain it was Alabama, but I digress. After the usual small talk ended, Jayson's jovial attitude turned somber as he asked how my investigation into potential additional embezzlement was going. There was a conspicuous pause as I froze at Jayson's simple question, which prompted Jayson to ask it again.

I wasn't quite sure how I should answer his question. If I told him what I had found, he might scold me for talking to people in direct contravention of his explicit orders and think I'd been wasting time on a wild goose chase. If I said I hadn't found anything yet, he might question my abilities. In the end, I decided to tell him that I had not found anything at that time. As I watched Jayson's reaction to my statement, I could not help but get the feeling that he was not buying it. There was something in his demeanor that made me believe he knew more than he was letting on. However, after I explained that I had not found any suspicious outflows of money to any personal accounts, he said he understood, and asked that I continue searching. The conversation then turned to a discussion of personnel matters, such as my upcoming end-of-year review and what conferences I was planning to attend in the new year so we could submit a budget for them now.

By the time the meeting was scheduled to end, I felt a massive wave of relief as I stood to exit Jayson's office. As I was walking to the door, Jayson reminded me that the "special assignment" was not just my top priority, but it was my only priority. After I said I understood, Jayson then repeated his prior admonition to keep my investigation secret from everyone, and to report any findings immediately to him, and him alone. Finally, he said: "And I want a report, a writeup, regardless of whether you found something or not– a written report in the next week–

okay?" I was just about to cross the threshold of the door, but then turned and said I would get him a report within the week. At that moment, just getting both of my feet outside of his office with my job still intact, felt like a major accomplishment.

For the second time in a week, I went back to my desk and stared blankly at my monitor, lost over what to do next. I knew Jayson had either guessed correctly, or more likely, had heard I was conducting my scheduled audit. Whether Jayson knew or not didn't matter, as I knew continuing the audit would be tantamount to career suicide, at least for South Lake and probably Peaked as well. So again, I sat in my cheap plastic chair tucked in my claustrophobic cubicle thinking of ways to approach this investigation. Eventually I began to just randomly pull up accounts and review the payment histories to see if there was anything that seemed odd or stood out to me. This lasted for about two hours with nothing noteworthy, not to my surprise, as it was a rather simplistic and hopeless approach. Surely a sophisticated, heck, even an average intelligence embezzler would have structured their illegal activity in such a way that nothing would seem odd just by looking at payment histories.

Lunchtime was a welcome reprieve from my mind-numbing search of accounts; however, as I stood in line waiting to order my usual sub sandwich at Rhino Shoppe, my thoughts wandered back to Account 44-56-7289-01. In particular, what stood out for me was that Nick Stern did not seem at all surprised or even concerned when I mentioned suspicious transactions in connection with the account. Instead, he seemed concerned with saying too much and, if I was being honest with myself, even came off as paranoid. He did mention there was something suspicious, but not so much related to the account; instead more of an overall suspiciousness. At least he had given me a lead with Javed and then, for reasons I didn't know, the name of some barely known sci-fi / fantasy author. I knew there was something there with this R&D account and, after quickly scarfing down my sub sandwich, rushed back to my desk, where I resumed looking into Account 44-56-7289-01.

Previously, I had looked at the account and noticed the tremendous growth over the prior year which had led to the conversation with Nick. However, what I had not done prior to that day was to look at how the funds in the account were being removed. Looking at the transfer of funds out of the account, there were two things that stood out immediately. First, the transfers were not consistently being made each month, but instead happened only a few times– three to be exact. The second thing was that the transfers were in large, round lump sums, with two transfers of $35,000 in July and another for $200,000 in September. This seemed quite odd for an internal account, especially a research and development account.

My experience was that these types of accounts typically operated with minimal carried over balances, meaning that funds deposited into the account were usually withdrawn within the next month, if not days. This type of activity makes sense, at least to me, when you consider that R&D needs to invest in projects it is developing, so any funds it receives are usually spent within a short period of time. In fact, sometimes funds are spent before the money even hits the account, leaving a debt that must be repaid immediately. However, in Account 44-56-7289-01, there was over $900,000 in funds, more than three-fourths of what was deposited, still in the account, just sitting there unused after twelve months. There was definitely something off about this; however, it did not look like embezzlement, since the money coming in was just sitting in the account. As such, the account seemed to be a dead-end for purposes of the "special project" and I frustratingly decided to revisit looking into individual accounts for suspicious activities.

Around 3:00 pm, as a dull pain in my eyes set in from staring at the screen, I received an email from Javed Agarwal. "Finally, a response" I thought excitedly, as I opened the message. Javed's email was brief; he stated he had been out of the office and requested I set up a call for the following day if I still wanted to discuss. I immediately scheduled the call for the same time the following day and then, wishing to end on a high note, decided to leave the office and go to the gym. As I walked to the elevator bank, I saw Paige approaching, carrying her large tan purse with a portion of her laptop slightly sticking out of the top. I smiled at her, to which she returned a small half-smile, but then noticeably avoided making eye contact, while turning her body so that her back was facing me as she looked down at her phone.

When the elevator doors opened, I motioned for her to enter, which she did, choosing a spot in the back left corner, while I stood in the middle. As the doors shut, I asked her how it was going, to which she replied blankly "Fine", not even attempting to look up from her phone. When the elevator doors opened again, I walked out but could tell that Paige was waiting till I was fully out to exit the elevator herself. It was clear she did not want to talk to me, and for whatever reason even seemed to be upset, or possibly mad at me. It was odd behavior, not because we were close or even friends, but because we had worked on the same floor for two plus years, during which we had seen each other in the elevator, out at lunch, and even at a few official, and some unofficial, company happy hours, without issue. Paige had always been cordial, even friendly with me on each of these occasions.

The drive to the gym as well as the first ten minutes on the treadmill were spent thinking about what might have caused Paige's attitude to change. As my shoes scraped repetitively against the moving track beneath my feet, I re-examined the events of the past few days to see if there was a clue I had missed, but nothing stood out. In fact, I could not recall even seeing her since I asked her for a contact in R&D and on that occasion, she was friendly as ever, even giving me Nick's name. "Could it be related to Nick?" I wondered, as I slowly began to notice the man on the treadmill three down from me.

He was taller than normal, maybe six-two, and stocky, but something about his build conveyed the impression muscle, not fat, lay beneath the skin. He had a shaved head, dark brown stubble lining his mouth and neck, pronounced cheekbones, and his left arm was completely covered in tattoos. He was wearing a loose navy T-shirt, black shorts, and what appeared to be black dress socks. Aside from the socks, he looked very normal for the gym, only I had never seen him there before, and as I tried to observe him out of the corner of my eye, I couldn't help feeling he was doing the same thing to me. Even though there were still twenty minutes left on the treadmill, I punched down on the screen's red button, which brought the moving track to a hasty stop. Then I briskly walked to the back left corner of the gym where the yoga mats were laid out on the floor and started doing crunches.

Within five minutes, I noticed the man was working on the leg press, which gave him a clear view of where I was, and then five minutes after that he was on the pull-up bar, no further than ten feet away from me. As he lowered his body after each pull-up, I could again sense he was looking not just in my section, but right at me. Finished with crunches, I skipped the rest of my workout, left the workout room, and headed down the hall to the locker room where I quickly changed my shirt, leaving my sweaty shorts on, grabbed my bag and rushed out of the locker room, not wanting to be in there a minute longer than needed. As I walked by the glass windows lining the workout room, I saw the same man who had followed me standing next to the rack full of weights located at the front of the room, and as I strode past, we made eye contact. I continued walking swiftly toward the exit, and broke eye contact with the man as I focused on the doors in front of me which would serve as my escape. Despite not looking back at the workout room, I was confident the man was still watching me as I pushed open the chrome handle opening the glass doors to the outside.

I raced home where, rather than taking the usual post-gym shower, I turned off all the lights in my apartment and sat peering out of my window blinds facing the street below. There I sat, on one of my two kitchen stools for over half an hour, watching the street below my apartment before it occurred to me— I had no idea what I was actually looking for, as I did not know what vehicle the man drove, nor if he was alone, or if there were others. Oddly, I began to feel much better as I thought about how clueless I was and about how absurd it was for me to just glare out my window like some crazy person in a movie. I abandoned my street- watching and went for a shower, then made dinner, which I subsequently ate alone on my little couch designed for two, and mindlessly watched a baking show on Netflix. Other than the gym, it was the same nightly routine I had been having for the past six months. A schedule initially born of depression after the break-up had become a habit.

The next morning, as I was placing the coffee filter in my coffee pot, the image of the mysterious man watching me flashed back like a waking nightmare. It was an image I could not shake as I dressed for work and then drove into the office. By the time I sat down at my desk, the irrational side of me was sure that someone was following me, not just yesterday at the gym, but even on my drive to the office that morning. These thoughts were being valiantly fought by the logical side of my mind which questioned why someone would follow me. As both the logical and illogical sides of my emotions fought it out, I opened my daily calendar and realized that I had a meeting with Javed scheduled for that afternoon. The irrational side of my brain thought that perhaps Javed had something to do with why I felt I was being followed, a thought the rational side of my brain failed to dispute.

This intrusive thought then raised its own question of why, followed by its own answer that Javed was embezzling money through the R&D GAIGE account. This idea festered and grew as I read through my morning batch of emails until the breaking point at which time this far-fetched idea became a plausible hypothesis. The more I thought about it, the less implausible it seemed, since I was investigating embezzlement, after all. By 10:00 am, I found myself sending an email to Alex asking if he could send me the names associated with the three accounts which received payments – two for $35,000 in July and another for $200,000 in September – from Account 44-56-7289-01. I purposely left Javed Agarwal's name out of my email, as I did not want to give out any more information than I needed to in case my hypothesis was correct. True to his reputation, Alex responded promptly within 10 minutes.

Good morning,
See below for requested information:

Account: 621555789
Bank: Deutsche Republik Banc, A.G.

Name on Account: Kruspe, H. Oliver

Account: 78783421
Bank: Bank of Grindelwald, Cayman Islands Branch
Name on Account: West-Higgins, Meredith

Account: 86753089
Bank: Bank of Lewiston (Idaho)
Name on Account: Jennifer Taylor and Patrick McCann

A wave of relief floated over me as I realized Javed's name was not associated with any of the three accounts. I then did a quick internet search for the names associated with the accounts which received money without anything noteworthy to show for it. Meredith West-Higgins, the owner of the account which received $200,000 in September, was the President and CEO of BrightArt Capital Partners, a joint venture which invested in smaller start-up media companies. Nothing came back for Jennifer Taylor, but there was a LinkedIn account for Patrick McCann which was rather bare, listing him as a graduate of Georgia Tech with a B.S. in computer science and a job history showing prior stints at IBM and Oracle, but no jobs since 2019.

The search for Oliver Kruspe returned similar results, although, while he did not have a LinkedIn account, there was a photo of him with some other members of Oracle at the ACM Symposium on Operating Systems Principles conference as well as a paper from the same conference titled 'pAInted: Transforming Artificial Intelligence into a Creative Engine for Human-Independent Artistic Generation.' While the lack of information on these people seemed a bit odd and probably should have set off some alarm bells, I was more focused on Javed not being linked to the payments and thus, my still being able to meet with him. It felt like forever till 3:00 pm arrived, but once it did, I immediately called Javed's number.

"Hello, Javed Agarwal here," he said almost immediately after I finished dialing.

"Hi, Javed, is now still a good time to talk," I asked.

"Yes, now is fine; however, I do have a hard stop at 3:30 as I have another call then," he replied. "Still catching up on work; after a week away on holiday, there is a lot to do."

"Of course, no doubt" I agreed, and, knowing my time was limited, immediately launched into my question. "Anyway, I am working on something, and the name GAIGE came up when talking to Nick Stern, and he said I should talk to you if I wanted to know more about it. And the reason I wanted to talk to you, is so that I could learn a little more about what GAIGE is, if you don't mind explaining it to me?"

"Well, that could take some time to explain it all," he replied, and I could hear the discomfort in his voice as it seemed he did not want to discuss it in detail. "Is there anything in particular you want to know about it, are you familiar with programming or have a background in computer science?"

"No, no background in computer science and can't say I know much about the subject– no more probably than the next person," I responded. "But I don't need to know how GAIGE works, at least I don't think I do; I'm just trying to understand what it is, if you could give, like a high-level overview of it?"

"Alright, I will do my best. GAIGE, which as you might know stands for Global AI Generating Enterprise, is an advanced proprietary machine learning program which we are hoping can be further enhanced and transformed into a generative artificial neural network, or as you probably have heard of it, artificial intelligence, or just A.I. for short."

"Uh huh, um, what do you mean by machine learning?"

"I guess the simplest way to describe it is a computer program learning from experiences in doing tasks that improves with experience," Javed said and probably sensing I was lost, continued. "Essentially, a program classifies data based on developed models and then makes predictions based on those models."

"Oh, and is that what GAIGE is, it is making predictions based on models?"

"There is more to it, but yes, in the simplest terms that is what it is designed to do."

"Interesting," I lied, not because it was not so, but instead because I had no idea what Javed just described, so could not tell if it was interesting, important, or what. After a moment of silence, I asked "So then, what type of predictions is this thing making?"

"Good question," said Javed, and I could tell he was already slightly annoyed with having to explain things to me. "GAIGE is an advanced program that isn't limited to one specific dataset or type of modeling. It is capable of analyzing almost any information you give it, whether that be weather or financial data, political polls, written works, shopping patterns, etcetera, and then based on simple modeling, generate predictions that align with the information entered and what you need it to do; so long as the right models are in place, of course."

"Ah, interesting," I said, and this time meant it.

"Yes, very much so," Javed said. "Now does that answer your question or is there anything else you need?"

"Well, it definitely helps knowing what GAIGE is," I replied before pausing briefly to think over everything Javed just said. I could tell by his question that he was hoping there was nothing else, but as I was re-examining everything I had just heard, one question crept into my mind. "But I do have one question: Is GAIGE currently in development or production, and if the latter, is it generating revenue?"

"Good question— it is somewhat both. We are using it in production of sorts— kind of a beta test— which generates a modest amount of revenue; however, we are still working on it, trying to further refine it in the background."

"Okay, and... then how is it generating revenue?" I queried, running my right hand through my hair as my brain struggled to process everything Javed had just said. "Are you, is Peaked selling the service to data analytic or consulting firms or the like?"

"No, although we could probably do that, but I believe

there is another group in the company who is already providing that service," Javed responded. "GAIGE is currently being developed and used for content creation—"

"Content creation," I blurted out without realizing I had interrupted him.

"Yes, content creation," Javed replied with a note of frustration in his voice. "GAIGE is being used to create stories, books, videos, and other forms of entertainment, although it currently is limited to written media, like novels, children's books, and scripts, with some song lyric writing also."

"Wow, that sounds amazing, but, umm, how is the program creating these stories? Is it from scratch or something else, because you mentioned modeling being part of this, right?"

"Correct, there are a number of models involved. But the program is quite simple, really. GAIGE analyzes the content of all the literary works uploaded to Peaked – all the short stories, novels, comics, children's books, and the like – and then advanced algorithms work to analyze the content to develop patterns and themes which are then used to generate new content. It is not quite at the level of artificial intelligence like you might be thinking, but it is rather advanced for machine learning in terms of what it can analyze, understand as patterns, and then generate based off that information."

"Wait, wait, so you're saying GAIGE is generating new works based on works that are already on Peaked's site?"

"Yes, that is correct," Javed responded. His attitude

had changed, as he now sounded more upbeat and happier to talk about what GAIGE was doing. "It is ingesting all the information from the works it has access to, then it analyzes the information, and finally produces new content based on pre-established developed models, and it does all of this in real-time, in a matter of moments. Take a romance novel which may have taken someone months to write; it can write, edit, and format in under five minutes. It can even design the book cover and start the advertising campaign."

"Amazing, just amazing, I can't believe you developed this, it just seems so impressive."

"Actually, I did not develop GAIGE. It was developed by some other people at Peaked. Oliver Kruspe, Patrick McCann, and Olivia Winston, I believe, were the ones who developed it, but they left the company a little while back. I was brought in to run the program when Pat and Olivia announced they were leaving, after Oliver had already left to pursue something else. Anyway, I apologize; however, I must go – a week of work to get back to."

"Okay, sure, but before you do, I do have one more question," I rushed to say before he hung up the phone. "In speaking with Nick Stern, he mentioned A.W. Bucher. Is that someone attached to GAIGE, did they create it, or something like that?"

"A.W. Bucher, haha, yes A.W. is linked to GAIGE, but no, *they* did not create it; actually quite the opposite. GAIGE created A.W. Bucher; that is, it is one of the test authors we created to see if the books GAIGE has created can be sold to the public. The first name A.W. actually stands for Artificially Written, and Bucher is German for Books, or at least that is what I've heard, so the author's name is actually Artificially Written Book! I believe this was the brainchild of Oliver before he left; he always liked to sneak his native German into projects whenever possible. I think he thought it was clever and maybe even funny, as probably only a German would. But getting back to A.W., it isn't completely artificial, there is a whole team dedicated to the initial creation process that GAIGE then utilizes, as well as other teams which handle managing the A.W. as a personality. So, actually, I believe I might have misspoken a moment ago. GAIGE did not create A.W., Oliver did, but the books that A.W. is publishing – those are mostly the work of GAIGE, with some help from a creative team, as I mentioned."

"What, that is—".

"Apologies, I do not mean to cut you off, but as I mentioned, I must go," Javed impatiently said, interrupting me. "If you need more information about how GAIGE was created, perhaps you can get in touch with Oliver, Patrick, or Olivia – they created it. I really just try to keep it running while I learn about it myself. Anyhow, all of the best, cheers."

"Yes, thank you for taking the time to speak with me," I said right before the line went dead.

So now I knew the truth about A.W. Bucher, or at least I thought I did. It was an amazing thing to think about, a non-sentient computer program creating art, such as writing a book. Although, from what Javed said, it seemed like there was still some human intervention in the process. I wondered how much of the writing is done by a machine and how much is done by a person, or more likely a committee of people? As this question lingered, I went to the Peaked site and again looked up *The Weeping Moon* by A.W. Bucher. I decided to buy the electronic version of the book and began reading. Twenty pages in, and nothing stood out for me. The book itself wasn't awful, nor was it that great, as the characters were too one dimensional and poorly developed, the plot itself unoriginal. Stopping for a moment to think, I remembered the book had a rather high 7.9 out of 10 rating. It seemed way too high of a rating for a book which seemed like an amalgamation of other more notable works.

I scrolled down the webpage until I found the reviews, which I proceeded to read in chronological order. The first thing I noticed was that the first set of reviews were all entirely positive. Additionally, while the text in each review was different, it seemed the format – three to four sentences with between 20 and 25 words in total length – and sentiment were the same across the reviews. This was sharply contrasted with the more recent reviews, which were mostly negative to indifferent, with a varying number of sentences and words being provided by each reviewer to describe their rating. The contradiction in reviews was baffling, but not beyond the realm of belief. It could very well be that the initial reviewers actually enjoyed the story and wrote only what was needed to describe their rating, while the more recent reviewers wanted to differentiate themselves, so as to sound like enlightened critics; thus, wrote more than was needed. I remembered having thought the same thing before and felt like I was running in circles.

That was until I looked back through the first ten reviews again and realized that all of them were written on the same day – August 12th. That seemed at the very least to be odd and at the most to be downright suspicious. "August, August, what is it about August of last year...of course, the payments for Account 44-56-7289-01," I thought to myself. I scrolled up to the top of the page and clicked to expand the details section for *The Weeping Moon*, when I saw it – release date: August 12. The reviews were written on the same day the book was released; this was way more than coincidence. On a hunch, I then clicked on the links to the other books which were recommended for me on the page. Of the five books I reviewed, four – *The Killing Time* by Lance McColl, *Saint Raphael's Curse* by Nadia Castellino, *Scripted Reality* by M.L. Raohut, and *Living the Past Over* by Art I. Chosha – had reviews that were written on the same day as the book was released. Each of these four books also was rated 7.5 or higher with the initial reviews being much more positive and favorable than the most recent reviews.

RUNNING SCARED

I now was pretty sure that I was onto something with my investigation. Thinking back on my conversation with Javed, I decided to begin writing down notes on the little yellow legal notepad sitting on my desk. I was determined to capture as much of what Javed said, word-for-word, as possible before I began to forget any part of the conversation. As I frantically scribbled my notes, I could not shake the questions which kept popping up in my mind. "Is this legal?" "Who is monitoring GAIGE?" "Can this even be profitable?" By the time I was finishing my third page of notes, these questions had completely consumed my thoughts to the extent they were blocking out all other thoughts. Since it was past 4:00 pm, I decided to duck out a little early, and headed to the gym for a good run on the treadmill to clear my head.

Similar to the prior day, when I arrived at the gym there were only a couple of other people in the workout room. This wasn't too surprising as it was not yet five o'clock, and most people were either still working or stuck in traffic. I grabbed the treadmill on the far-right corner, near the window and furthest away from the center of the room where people tended to congregate. Twenty minutes into my run, and most of the questions and thoughts about GAIGE were finally beginning to leave my mind. It was at this point that I started to look around at the areas nearest to me and that is when I saw him, the man from the prior day, running on another treadmill only three down from mine. I immediately averted my eyes upon realizing it was the same man. It seemed like no coincidence seeing him here again, running so close to me, and for the second time I felt like he was discreetly watching me, keeping track of my movements.

A sudden panic overtook me, and I could feel my chest tightening with each exasperated breath. As fear set in, it took everything in me to avoid tripping on the treadmill; however, I kept running for another ten minutes without any noticeable change in the man's actions. A burning pain started to take root deep in my calf muscles and I knew I could not keep on running much longer. I punched the red button in the center of the treadmill display, grabbed my keys from the plastic box that protruded off the side of the display and immediately headed out of the workout room and gym, leaving my bag with my work clothes in the locker room. Once I was in the car and began to back up in the parking lot, a feeling of relief came over me. I was looking all around me, out the driver and passenger side windows, in the rear-view mirror and, of course, in front of my car as I exited the parking lot and started to drive home.

It was twenty minutes past five and the sun was beginning to disappear into the horizon, setting the sky aglow with pink, red, and orange hues mixed in with the white clouds in the darkening blue sky. My apartment was approximately twenty miles away from the gym in Stallings and involved a pleasant drive down a two-lane road past a mixture of residential neighborhoods and rural farmland that lay some thirty minutes south of Charlotte. There were gyms closer to my apartment, but this was the first gym I joined when I moved to town, and I had not found any better since. And while it was close to my old apartment where my ex still lived, I was not in too much danger of running into her, as she managed to avoid the area as a whole.

I was switching between watching the road in front of me and the changing sky above when a feeling that I was being watched, eerily similar to the one I had in the gym, started to grow inside. A dark-colored muscle car, which looked like either a Dodge Charger or Ford Mustang, was approaching fast from the rear. It was difficult to fully make out the car, let alone the person driving it, as the car's headlights made it almost impossible to see anything other than the two blinding circles of yellowish-white light that were filling the interior of my car with a white glow. The car stayed behind me, seemingly right on my rear bumper for about five minutes before slowly backing off only a few feet. I was more than ten minutes from my apartment and beginning to panic from the thought of being followed.

The car followed me down the winding Tilley Morris Road and then, taking the first hand turn at the roundabout, continued down Chestnut Lane. It continued to follow me as we passed by Strawberry Road and Fairforest

Drive, street names that normally conjured up pleasant images, but in this moment signaled the end was near. I sped up, slowed down, and even began to swerve a little as though I were drunk, hoping that any of this might cause the car behind me to fall back or even better, pass me, but it never did. The black muscle car matched each speed change and movement as its distance from my bumper remained unchanged. After the car matched my fifth and last speed change, I knew I had to try something else, as I could not risk the car following me all the way back to my apartment, and the driver learning where I lived. Taking control of my nerves, I remembered passing Hidden Cove Lane a few miles back and suddenly a thought burst into my mind.

There was a gravel road coming up on the right in about a mile which I decided would be my best option at losing the car. The turn was approaching fast, but I continued at the same speed of about fifty-five miles an hour. As my lights quickly illuminated the white pole holding up the white box sign with "Goose Creek Airport" written in white on it, I pushed down on the brake pedal and ripped my steering wheel almost 180 degrees to the right. I felt the wheels of the car slipping on the road and my body was thrown back and to the left in my seat. As I heard rocks being thrown up and away from the car, I straightened the wheel and focused on navigating down the winding, darkened road. Looking in my rearview mirror, it seemed the mysterious car had not made the turn, since the lights of the car had disappeared, leaving nothing but darkness behind. I continued driving for another half-mile or more before pulling off into a small open dirt patch where I turned off all my lights, but kept the engine running, while I waited to see if the car was coming down the road. I remained like that, clenching my steering wheel, ready to take off at any moment, for ten of the longest minutes of my life before I decided it was safe to head home.

I drove back down the gravel path toward the main road, then stopped to make sure there were no vehicles coming from either direction. Not seeing any lights, I turned back onto the road and resumed driving toward home, when after a few moments, I saw the lights of an oncoming car approaching fast. I immediately tensed up and, as the lights got brighter, I recognized that the vehicle approaching me was the same one that had been following me. When it got closer, I was finally able to discern what it was — a metallic blue Ford Mustang. A moment later, it passed me traveling at least seventy miles an hour in the opposite direction.

Not wanting to be caught, I sped up to at least eighty miles an hour, hoping that if the Mustang turned around to follow, at least I would have put some considerable distance between us before it turned. I continued to speed down the two-lane road for nearly the entire distance before I finally slowed down to turn left onto the side street off which my apartment was located. No one had followed me as far as I could tell but that did not relieve my fears. I decided it best to park in an open spot in the parking lot for the apartment on the other side of the street from mine. I exited the car and rushed across the street and sprinted up the stairs to my apartment, where I sat at my dining room window watching the street below. After a half hour had passed, without any sign of the Mustang, or anyone else for that matter, passing through, I finally headed off to my bedroom for a shower before going to bed.

Needless to say, I could not fall asleep that night. At first, I was kept awake by the dread that at any moment, someone, perhaps the mystery man from the gym, would bust through the front door and then murder me before I had a chance to exit through my bedroom window. As the minutes, then hours passed, these frightening thoughts seemed less and less likely to occur, so that by about 3:00 am I was barely even thinking about it anymore. Instead, I was focused on the whys: why was I being followed, and why would someone want to scare, or worse, harm me? I could not help but think it was somehow tied to Account 44-56-7289-01 and the GAIGE program. But what was so secretive and so important about this account and GAIGE that someone, or some group of people would want to follow and intimidate me? These questions occupied my thoughts and lingered throughout the rest of the night until the alarm on my phone started buzzing at 7:15 am.

THE DAY AFTER LAST NIGHT

Despite all that had happened and my utter lack of sleep, I moved effortlessly through my morning routine of making coffee, showering, putting on my usual button up shirt and blue slacks, checking the day's weather and personal emails on my phone, and of course, grabbing two pieces of gum, so as to not break my fast, before leaving my apartment. In stark contrast to the prior night, everything proceeded remarkably smoothly that morning, so much so that I arrived at work ten minutes earlier than usual and was already caught up on emails by 9:30 am. Without much to do, I sat back in my flimsy, uncomfortable work chair with its cheap plastic frame and began to think back over what had happened. At first, my thoughts focused entirely on what happened during the drive home; however, as time passed, I started to question my own memories as to whether the events I remembered even happened, or at least occurred the way I thought they did. Feeling my grip on reality fading slightly, I changed my focus to the investigation. I grabbed my notebook from the locked desk drawer and began to read over the notes I had jotted down in my left-handed scrawl. The notes left more questions than answers about the GAIGE R&D account.

Javed was able to tell me what GAIGE is, so there was some progress on that front. But Javed seemed to be someone who came into the process late, and his usefulness in terms of the investigation probably had already hit its limits. He did offer three names – Patrick, Oliver, and Olivia – who undoubtedly would be great sources, perhaps even explaining away all the questions. However, there was one major problem: all three were no longer with the company, and all attempts to locate them via outside sources had produced zip, zilch, nada, absolutely nothing. I was becoming frustrated at the thought of having so many questions and no way of obtaining any answers. The transactions and circumstances surrounding account 44-56-7289-01 and this GAIGE program had become a mystery, one that was now impacting my personal life, and one which I felt the desperate need to solve.

My head sank down in despair and I closed my eyes while I began to run my fingers aggressively through my hair in frustration. The questions still outnumbered the answers; in fact, there might now be even more unanswered questions than there were at the start of the investigation. After a few prolonged and deep breaths, I opened my eyes and saw the answer staring up at me from the middle of the notepad – Nick Stern. I immediately searched and found the prior email from him and called the number he listed in the email. After about eight rings, I hung up and tried calling again, this time waiting until I heard Nick's voice say, "You have reached the voicemail of Nick Stern, please leave a message." Having no luck with his personal number, I logged onto Peaked's employee homepage and searched for Nick's name in the directory; however, nothing came back. As a last result, I replied to Nick's original email from over a week before, but within a minute of sending an email asking him to give me a call, I received an auto generated email which said:

Your email is being returned as undeliverable.

Please check the spelling and address. If this problem continues, please contact Peaked Information Technology Services at 800-555-0101.

"What the heck is going on?" I blurted out in frustration. It was almost as if Nick had left the company, but I knew from experience that even when an employee does leave, it usually takes at least two weeks for all the systems to update. It had only been nine or ten days since I spoke with him, and now, here he was apparently removed from all of Peaked's systems. "Great, just more questions," I thought. There were two things I did know: first, I was not going to get any answers just sitting there, and second, Paige Caruso knows Nick, so maybe she could tell me what happened and, more importantly, how to get in touch with him.

I pushed my chair back from the desk, stood up, and walked down the corridor to Paige's cubicle, which was located by the glass windows at the far end of the room. As I approached, I could see her strawberry blonde hair peeking out over the top of the cubicle wall. Turning around the corner of the wall, I noticed that she was scrolling through a newspaper article about the English Royal Family on one screen while the other screen displayed her open email inbox. "Good, she isn't busy," I said to myself.

"Hi, Paige, how is it going," I said.

"Okay," she replied curtly as her body appeared to tense up.

"So, I was wondering if you might have a moment?"

Paige did not respond. Instead, she continued scrolling through the article, but it seemed she was aggressively trying to avoid me. Her face moved closer to the screen, while her left hand jerked the mouse around making a noticeable scratching sound as it slid across her desk.

"Apologies, I don't mean to interrupt, but might you have a second to chat?"

"No, not for you," she replied.

"Oh! Well, look, if there is something I've done, I'm sorry, but I really need to talk to you about Nick."

"Nick," she scoffed before turning to finally look at me. "Go away... just go away now."

"Look, I don't know what's the matter," I started to say as I raised my arms and took a couple steps backward. "But really, I need just a moment, and then I'll be out of your hair."

"Go away!" She repeated but this time with hostility in her voice.

"Okay, I will, but why are you upset at me – I mean we haven't even talked in a couple of weeks – so why, what have I done?"

"Huh," she sneered. "You are the reason all of this happened, you got Nick fired and then you have the audacity to come over here and ask about him. I mean what nerve on you."

"Fired," I exclaimed in confusion.

"Yes, fired," she replied. "Why would I ever want to talk to you after what you did?"

"Look, look, I'm sorry, but I have no idea what you are talking about, I didn't, I didn't—"

"You got Nick fired," she said, interrupting me. "Nick talks to you one day and then, poof, he's fired the next day. Of course you got him fired. That is why people don't talk to Audit, and I should have known better."

"Look, I swear to you, I did not get Nick fired," I pleaded. "In fact, until you said something, I had no idea he had been fired. I swear, this is all news to me."

"Well, it isn't coincidence; he talks to you one day and then is let go the next day."

"Listen, I can't fire anyone— seriously— I don't have that power. I don't think anyone in audit has anything close to that power. And even if I did, I did not fire him. There is no reason why I would. Hell, he helped me by answering some questions, something about which I need to talk with him again. And I was hoping you could help with that."

"Unbelievable," she uttered while shaking her head. "Just unbelievable."

"Look, that is the truth, the honest truth, I did not get him fired, and honestly, I had no idea he was let go or who would have done that," I continued. "I mean, really, if I had gotten him fired, why would I be coming over here to ask you about getting in touch with him?"

"Well, you won't have any luck with that," Paige said.

"What do you mean," I inquired.

"Nick's gone," she said bluntly as her eyes began to swell and tears formed around the lower edges of her eyes as her initial rigid demeanor had given way to despondency.

"He's gone? What do you mean he's gone. Where did he go?"

"After he was fired, he called me to let me know and said he didn't know what to do. He didn't want to go home to his wife and kids— he didn't know what he would say to her. So, some other people here and I left work early and met him for drinks the day he was fired. After a couple drinks and talking things over, when we left the bar he seemed in good spirits, as good as you could be, I guess, given the circumstances. But the next day, Kendra Reece, from Nick's department, texted me to say she heard from Nick's wife that he had committed suicide."

"Oh, my, wow!" I exclaimed, shaking my head in disbelief. "What? How?"

"Apparently he told his wife he was going for an early morning run and then went to a nearby park, where he shot himself in the head."

"Jesus, that's awful."

"Yeah, yeah, it is," Paige said. "But when we were out drinking, Nick said that he had talked with you about something, something he probably should not have, and that after doing so he was fired. So naturally, he blamed you. He was saying at the bar that you had told people that he was out there talking about this thing that he shouldn't have been talking about, and that is why he was fired on the spot. I mean he said he wasn't even allowed to pack up his things, he arrived at work in the morning, and his boss and a security guard met him in the lobby and said he was let go and that they would send his stuff to his house, but he was not to set foot in the building."

"Damn, that's shitty," I replied as a question came to mind about something Paige had said. "Wait, you said you got drinks with him. Nick was in Charlotte?"

"Yes, he was over at Peaked's South Park location. It's off Fairview I think," Paige answered wiping a tear from her cheek. "I actually knew him from our days together at Lowe's, and then we both came here about the same time, before he decided to go over to Peaked."

"Oh, I'm so sorry, honestly I am, and you probably don't want to hear this right now, but I had nothing to do with him being fired, I swear."

Paige nodded her head which I hoped meant she believed me but doubted it deep down. Feeling incredibly awkward at that moment and wanting to avoid saying something inappropriate, I turned and walked back to my desk. The rest of the day and night went by uneventfully followed by an equally uneventful following morning. At 12:50 pm the next day, I returned from lunch to see I had a few new emails, including one from Jayson. I immediately opened the email which said:

Let's meet in my office today at 3. Let me know if you cannot make it.

Best,

-J.

As I sat at my desk after reading Jayson's email, I could feel my nervousness increase with each passing minute. My chest and back tensed up, and my hands became noticeably drier, as the blood rushed back to my rapidly beating heart. "Shit, it's Friday, of course it is," I thought to myself. It was well known that South Lake, like many other companies, preferred to fire or lay people off on Fridays, especially Friday afternoons, without any warning. Apparently, firing people without warning on a Friday reduced the likelihood of retaliation or workplace violence, as offices are closed the following day.

A few minutes before three o'clock, I pushed back my chair and began to stand up before collapsing back into my chair. In the hour I had spent just staring vacuously at my cubicle wall, I had failed to realize how my tenseness had spread to the muscles in my legs, causing them to grow tight and stiff. On the second attempt, I was able to regain my balance and started to walk down the large corridor to Jayson's office. When I arrived, I could see his door was shut and the office was occupied by three people. Susan Henderson and the tall, thin, balding man from before were sitting on the opposite side of the desk from Jayson. They seemed to be engaged in a serious conversation, so I moved to stand next to an empty nearby cubicle, hoping to hide a bit while still maintaining a view of the office. I heard the sound of suction from Jayson's glass door as it opened, and Susan walked out of the office. Walking over to Jayson's office, I came face-to-face with the tall, thin man who was just then emerging from within. The man's eyes were sunken into his emaciated face, and there were dark patches under both eyes. As I stood there, I could not help but get the feeling the man was sizing me up, looking me over head-to-toe. A single, sharp shiver shot through my body as he continued standing in front of me, not moving an inch. "Excuse me," I said as I slid to my right and walked into Jayson's office without knocking.

"Hey, perfect timing," Jayson said as I sat down in the chair in front of his desk. I pretended to move my head to the right and left as though I were stretching so that I could use my peripheral vision to discreetly see what the tall, thin man was doing. However, as I strained to look, all I could see were the empty cubicles which lay outside the office. "So, how is the special assignment going?" Jayson asked, shifting his focus from the screen on his desk to me.

"Um, it's going," I replied.

"Okay," he said, nodding slightly. "Have you found anything, anything noteworthy or suspicious?"

"No, not really," I responded. "There were a couple of things I was looking into, but nothing right now that I would say looks like embezzlement."

"Okay, okay," he said, as his body started to rock in his chair. "And you're focused on this assignment and not working on the audit, right?"

"Yes, I haven't done anything with the audit since we last talked."

"Okay, okay, good," he said, his body continuing to

rock in the chair. He then shifted his gaze from me to a random spot on the empty right wall in his office. He continued gazing at the wall for a few seconds before he shifted his gaze back onto me, followed by a deep breath. "Okay, so I've heard that you may be looking into something over at Peaked. I don't know what it is, but apparently you are trying to talk to people over there about some accounts or something, I'm guessing it's part of your annual AML review for the year-end reports, maybe."

"Okay," I relented, as my entire lower body went completely numb from fear.

"Okay, you don't deny this, or okay, you understand what I said?"

"Both, I mean I know what you said and I'm not denying it," I replied. There did not seem a point in lying to him. As I figured it, if anything, lying would only give him more ammunition and put me at a greater disadvantage. Also, part of me hoped that he believed what I was doing was for the year-end reports, but it seemed he knew more than he was letting on. Perhaps his statements were offered up to see if I would correct him and volunteer more information.

"Okay, well, as I said, I don't know what it is that you are asking about over there, and I don't want to know," responded Jayson after a momentary pause. "But as I stated before, your only job right now is to look for possible embezzlement, not anything else, do you understand?"

"I do understand, but this..." I started to reply, but

decided against saying anything more about why I was looking into GAIGE. It was obvious that Jayson knew more, but there was no need for me to serve everything up to him on a platter. And luckily, it seemed Jayson was not paying enough attention at that moment to catch that I had stopped myself mid-sentence.

"Okay, just so we are all clear, when you leave this office, you will stop whatever it is you are doing, year-end reporting related or not, and you will focus only on the special assignment, looking for any signs of embezzlement, is that clear?"

"Yes, crystal clear," I replied.

"Okay, well that is all. I just wanted to level-set and make sure you understood you are only to be looking into one thing, possible embezzlement, until told otherwise, okay?"

"Yes, understood," I said, rising gingerly from the chair as sensation slowly returned to my lower body.

When I got back to my desk, the sense of relief I had felt at not being fired and still having my job was slowly replaced by fear. Jayson's warning about not continuing the investigation or speaking with anyone at Peaked echoed continuously in my head. I now knew that he was aware of what I was doing. I initially had thought that Paige informed him as a sort of retribution. However, this idea passed as it occurred to me that Nick was fired almost immediately after talking to me. Somehow, someone at Peaked or South Lake knew that Nick had told me about GAIGE and this same person, or someone else, had also informed Jayson and told him to pressure me to stop looking into it.

When I realized it was already 4:40 pm, I shut down my computer and headed home, resolved to let the investigation of GAIGE stop right then and there. And I was doing a good job of forgetting about everything until Sunday night. After a day spent running errands and working out, I decided to have a few drinks that night to relax. As I moved onto my third beer, the open questions regarding GAIGE came rushing back into my mind, filling all my thoughts. As I lay on the couch progressing on to my fourth beer, I decided that I could not stop the investigation, not after coming this far. Patrick McCann or Oliver Kruspe were the keys to understanding everything. And it occurred to me, there might be one more way to find them. But doing so would probably lead to word getting back to Jayson that I had not stopped the investigation. I figured it was a risk I would have to take.

PATRICK MCCANN

"How did you find me?" asked the voice on the other end of the phone. Patrick had a thick Boston accent which seemed like it was even more pronounced due to the noticeable hostility in his voice.

"I located you in the HR database" I replied.

"Yeah, but why were you looking for me, what is it that you want?" the voice shot back.

"Well, I'm working on something, a project, and GAIGE, Global AI Generating Enterprise, I believe is what it stands for, came up in my investigation" I responded, immediately kicking myself for saying it was an "investigation".

"Okay, and what does this have to do with me?"

"I was talking to Javed Agarwal, who currently runs GAIGE and, well, he couldn't answer a lot of my questions because, as he said, all he does is run it, he didn't create it. And then he mentioned I would need to speak to someone who knows more about it, someone who was around when it was created."

"And what does this have to do with me?" he asked again. He really was making me spell it out, which I found to be quite annoying.

"Well, Javed mentioned your name as well as another, an Oliver Kruspe."

"Then it sounds like maybe you should be talking to – [deliberate pause] – to this Oliver you mentioned," he replied, his inflection becoming aggressive and agitated.

"Yes, well, I tried finding Oliver but could not. It almost seems like he disappeared," I said, trying to keep my voice as calm as possible.

"Not surprising," he said.

"What do you mean?" I asked.

"Look, I don't like people calling me out of the blue. Especially people calling about work when I don't work there anymore. I mean how the hell did you even find me in the first place?"

"As I said before, I looked you up in the Peaked HR system. Your email and phone number were still listed in the back end of the system, even though you are not listed in the directory anymore."

"Shit, look, I can't talk about any of this to a reporter, to the public, to anyone," he said.

"Yes, but I'm not a reporter. As I mentioned, I work at South Lake Union Management Corporation. It is basically a subsidiary of Peaked, and I need help understanding GAIGE."

"I know what South Lake is, but I can't help you out on that," he said.

The sound on the other end of the line went dead silent. After a moment of listening to nothing but the sound of my own breathing, I realized that he had hung up on me. "Rude" I thought to myself. It was obvious from the moment Patrick first answered the phone that he did not want to talk. Part of me thought it best to just move on and do nothing more, while the other part of me—the part driven by curiosity and desire to solve the puzzle—wanted to call him back, press him to answer my questions. My curiosity won out, and while I was re-dialing the number, I thought about what to say. I knew it would need to be quick and it must grab his attention.

"I told you I can't talk, okay, so why don't you—".

"Look, wait, before you hang up, I know what GAIGE is," I said, interrupting him, hoping I had caught his attention. "I know it is more than just some advanced program designed to solve problems. It is actually some sort of machine learning program that is learning how to write, using books already on Peaked's site. That the goal of all of this is to have it create content, masquerading itself as human, that would then be sold to the public...novels, kids' books, that sort of thing."

"It is a lot more than just that."

"How do you mean?" I asked, feeling relief as I realized he hadn't hung up on me.

"You don't understand. I can't talk about this— no matter if I wanted to or not— [pause] and look, I do, I really do," he said, his voice beginning to crack a little.

"Yes, but I already know that GAIGE is using the materials, novels, books, stories, that are uploaded by authors into Peaked for sale as a means to learn and generate new material."

"That's just the tip of the iceberg. It is a lot, lot more complicated than just analyzing published books."

"Okay, how so?"

There was a long pause on the other end of the line. I began to worry that he might have hung up on me again. I wondered what he meant by saying there was more. I was struggling to think through what else it might be when I heard a deep exhale on the other end of the line.

"Okay, screw it," he said. "So, you are right. GAIGE is taking in all of the books that have been uploaded to Peaked and using that to teach itself writing. But that is just the start, as all it really has right now is a library of already published works. It doesn't have anything original. And it can't at this point, without humans– right? It still needs humans for original ideas. Or does it?"

"Are you asking me?" I asked.

"No, just being rhetorical, I guess" Patrick responded, his accent becoming much thicker, as he was undoubtedly getting more annoyed with me. A feeling that was mutual. "Anyway, as I was saying, originality was always, probably still is, the limitation of GAIGE ever since when we first designed it. It was incapable of original thought. It could write you a novel in the style of John Grisham, but it still needed a human to guide it, to give it direction for what the story would be, where it was going, and the like. The human element was going to limit how much GAIGE could be used, and thus, how much money it could make for Peaked. That was, until Oliver had the idea to capture human ideas in real-time, to go beyond just analyzing published works."

"I'm sorry, capturing ideas in real-time?"

"Yes, getting the ideas as they happen. Now obviously, we couldn't hook people up to the machine. First, the technology to read minds doesn't exist, or if it does, we didn't have it. Second, you would need people to agree to it and you would, most importantly, need to pay them. This was definitely a hard 'no' for the project, but I digress. Anyway, whatever we did, it needed to remain private. The public could not know, and we needed to ensure all, or nearly all, of the profits from sales remained with Peaked. So that is where BookSellF comes into play. You've heard of it, right?"

"Bookshelf, like where you put books," I asked.

"No, it sounds like it on purpose, but it's B-O-O-K-S-E-L-L-F, all one word, with the B, S and F capitalized" he replied, spelling out the name.

"Um, can't say I have heard of it."

"Yeah, I guess that makes sense. Well, it is pretty big with screenwriters and authors and the like. It is a website and application that assists people with writing. An author can go in, select different options, and the application will format their writing in real-time as they write. It allows writers to have a polished, finished item, whether it be a novel or kid's book, or screenplay at the end. It actually has a lot of neat features, but I digress. Anyway, there are two things people don't know about it. First, while it appears to be an independent site and application, it is, through a lot of complex legal mechanisms, owned by Peaked. Second, and perhaps even more important, is that BookSellF feeds into GAIGE. This means that, as a person is drafting their novel, that draft novel is showing up in GAIGE. GAIGE then can make changes to the character names, use a number of synonyms to change words, and re-order some of the text to make the novel appear original and unique. Then, once the human author's draft reaches a certain point, usually about 60% complete, GAIGE will populate the remainder of the novel using its learned library. The novel will then be copyrighted and published under one of a number of non-existent writers and sold to the public."

"Wow," I exclaimed in disbelief at what I just heard. "What you're saying is that GAIGE is stealing people's draft works and publishing before they have a chance to themselves?"

"Yup, that is what I'm saying, although not officially and you didn't hear it from me."

"But why? Why go to all this work and expense to develop not only GAIGE, but to set up a fake company and develop software that helps authors, while also stealing their ideas?"

"It's simple — money. See, currently, Peaked collects 55% of the proceeds on the sale of a book, with the author collecting the other 45% as royalties. For a $20 book that sells 100,000 copies, this means that Peaked collects one million, one hundred thousand dollars, while the author collects nine hundred thousand dollars. The nine hundred thousand dollars isn't exactly a lot for a company with revenues in the hundreds of billions range, but that is just for one book. Multiply that by, say 200, the average number of books with over 100,000 copies sold, and you have close to two-hundred million in revenue. So, just eliminating the author royalties on those books would bring in nearly two hundred million a year, and that is just a small fraction of the overall total of the profits they could realize publishing with GAIGE. If you expand this to nearly, if not all, of the books listed on Peaked, then you are talking billions of dollars of revenue going directly into Peaked's account. No royalty payments, no contract negotiations, no labor disputes, strikes, or anything of the sort that might come from dealing with humans."

"Damn," I burst out in dismay.

"Yes, and that is just the start. There are other applications like BookSellF; things like MotionCap for movies and Sound Studio X for musicians, which are doing the same thing – helping people create movies and songs, while at the same time taking those early versions and sending them to GAIGE to be spit back out to the public. Although both of these are still somewhat in their infancy, at least they were when I was – [pause] – when I left."

"Wow! So, soon it may be producing movies and songs. Amazing, just amazing."

"Yes, and it would be doing so by essentially stealing from other people, beating them to market so to speak," Patrick said before pausing. I sensed that he was debating whether to proceed.

Trying to persuade him to continue, I decided to ask, "but is there going to be enough material on these sites? I mean, it seems like these sites– like BookSellF– they would only be used by amateur writers, and probably not the best content for major publication, right?"

"You are probably right in some regard, but remember, GAIGE is able to build off the material it's learned from analyzing popular writers. So, it can take a story idea from some amateur and then mold the language, the style to match that of the greats – Stephen King, Fitzgerald, Hemingway, you name it – [pause] – and, well I've heard rumors, rumors that...," Patrick trailed off after the pause before suddenly stopping mid-sentence.

"What rumors?" I pressed.

"Well, there are rumors that Peaked isn't just relying on these creative sites, that they are actively hacking better known writers to steal their drafts right off their computers."

"What, how is that even possible?"

"I don't know," he replied briskly. "Like I said, they were just rumors, but, well, someone told me that Henry had hired some Eastern European hackers to see if they could get access to these authors' saved drafts on their computers. See, what you need to understand is that we– Henry, Rao, and I– but especially Henry, were under a lot of pressure to show that GAIGE could deliver the results people higher up were expecting. They, senior management that is, wanted a program that could write a book or create a song from scratch that they could then sell directly, without having to pay royalties to anyone outside of Peaked. But as I said before, GAIGE was not close to that point; it could not generate an original idea, so we needed other ways to do that."

"Damn, if that rumor is true, then that means, well you know," I said at a loss for words, not wanting to say anything over the phone about breaking the law in case our call was being monitored. Shifting back to what Patrick had just said, I asked: "Who is Henry?"

"Henry," Patrick stated with some confusion in his voice. "Oh yes, sorry, Heinrich Kruspe, but I called him Henry for short, although I don't think he liked it, but whatever. He preferred to be called Oliver, which is what I think you said earlier. Oliver was his middle name I believe, but he went by it here in the States because– well, you know– Heinrich isn't exactly a name that conjures up images of puppies and rainbows, right? Haha."

"I mean, I guess I could see wanting to go by a middle name," I said while looking over my notes to find my next question. There were still at least a dozen that I wanted answers to, but I decided to focus on figuring out who was involved. I figured that once more people were identified, then I would have more chances to ask questions and get answers, as Patrick did not seem ready or willing to answer many more questions. "So, I noticed there was a payment back in July made to a Bank of Lewiston account, account number ending in 089, that is listed in both your name and Jennifer Taylor. So first, who is Jennifer Taylor?"

"She is, she was – [sigh] – my wife," came Patrick's strained response.

"Oh, so sorry to hear," I said before taking a pause to let the air clear, as I was unsure what had just transpired. "And, I hate to ask, but there was a rather large payment from the GAIGE R&D account, about $35,000, that was made to the Bank of Lewiston account, could you tell me what this was for?"

"Look, I've said all I can," he replied. "I really have to go. Best of luck with this. I really do – [pause] – I hope you realize what you have gotten yourself into–this is the big leagues. Big time money means higher stakes and bigger risks, so I wish you the best."

The line went dead, which was becoming an all too common and frustrating occurrence. I wanted to ask him what he meant by the "higher stakes and bigger risks" part. Was this just a statement, or was he talking about how important GAIGE was, or was it something more ominous? The statement only reaffirmed that what had happened to me recently was not a figment of my imagination, that it was somehow all related. But I still needed more answers, and at this point, Patrick was my only lead left. I tried calling the number back a few times but each time the call ended after one ring.

I reviewed the notes I had taken during the call. Besides giving me a description of how GAIGE was creating new books, Patrick had also unintentionally given me Oliver's real first name. I immediately opened my browser and typed Heinrich Kruspe into the search engine. The second result listed was an apparent news article with Heinrich Kruspe in the headline. I clicked on the link which took me to what appeared to be a site for a German newspaper: The Augsburger Allgemeine, and there was the headline: *Anwohner Heinrich Kruspe kommt nach einem Autounfall in der Bundesstraße 2 ums Leben.* I copied and pasted the headline into an online translator which translated the headline as: Local man, Heinrich Kruspe, dies after one car crash on Bundesstraße 2. "Shit, it can't be– first Nick, and now this Heinrich guy," I thought to myself. It was becoming clear that these deaths were not coincidental, and someone was going to a lot of effort to make sure whatever secrets they held remained secrets. I was not certain that the man from the gym with the tattooed arm and the Ford Mustang from a few nights before were indeed following me, but any doubts I had were disappearing by the day.

Surprisingly, at that moment I was remarkably calm and collected. After more than two weeks of odd events causing hypervigilance, my nerves and emotions had become almost numb. For the first time in a while, I felt like my head was clear, allowing for the puzzle pieces to begin to come together. I opened a blank Word document on my computer and began to transcribe my notes from my worn notebook, supplementing them with events and other things I remembered, but had failed to write down. These notes would not just be for the police, but for the whole world, because people need to know, not just the headlines or a synopsis, but the whole story of what happened.

But just writing down what I discovered, and others told me was not going to be enough. I needed proof. Proof that GAIGE existed and how it worked, especially how it was getting the information it used to generate content. Unfortunately, what I needed—schematics and internal program documents—was well beyond what I had access to in my role. I needed someone to get the info for me, someone close to GAIGE, who would be willing to risk their career, and perhaps even their life, to get me the information. Until I found that person, I was essentially at a dead end.

However, my luck changed the afternoon of Friday, October 22nd, when I received the text: "I may have something you want regarding that thing you're looking into. Meet me at Freedom Park, tomorrow @ 7pm. Come alone." The text came from an unknown number. I ran through a list of people who may have sent it, which was not very long. Nick was dead. Paige did not seem to know anything. Patrick lived in Idaho, at least that was what came up when I dialed his number. And Javed worked in Peaked's main office in Denver. It seemed like this might be a trap, but since I was getting nowhere fast, I decided I would meet them, if nothing to relieve some of my curiosity.

ON DIRECT

Jamal al-Bashir sat in the small, wooden box at the front of the courtroom. He was flanked on his left by Judge Eriksson, whose seat was two feet higher than Jamal's, by design, to allow for the judge to have a commanding presence over the room. There was a small space just wide enough for two people to walk past on Jamal's right, before approaching the jury box occupied by the twelve jurors, composed of seven women and five men. Jamal had been alternating between facing the jury and the defense attorney, Preston Quarles, who stood at the podium located about ten feet away in the center of the courtroom as Jamal read from the letter. Upon finishing, he looked up from the eleven-page document in his right hand and sighed. Jamal hated speaking in public and was relieved to be finished reading aloud; however, this feeling was short-lived, as he began to dread what was to come next.

"Alright, now Mr. al-Bashir, how did you come to be in possession of the note you just read for the jury?"

"As I said, it was on the windshield of my car when I came out from work one day," Jamal responded.

"Okay, okay," Preston began as he moved from standing behind the podium toward the jury box. "And do you know who wrote this note and put it on your car?"

"No, no I do not," Jamal replied. He was tired of being asked this question. He had told the police repeatedly he did not know who wrote it. And as for the note being on his car's windshield, he told the police there were at least other people who drove nearly identical red Toyota High-landers who parked near him at work.

"But how can that be if you worked in the audit department and whoever wrote the note, it would seem, also worked in the audit department? It wasn't that big of a department, was it?"

"No, the audit team at South Lake was small. I basi-cally knew everyone there," Jamal began. "But the thing is, we were all new to the department. Back in November of last year, South Lake let go of the entire audit depart-ment, along with some other groups. There was a big re-structuring and downsizing at the time; even my old group was reduced. I was lucky enough to move from my old role in accounting into audit just after they let go of everyone."

"What about the letter and the envelope—was there any indication who may have written it?" Preston had stopped walking about six feet from the jury box and he looked directly at each juror. "Was there any name or other clue as to who wrote it?"

"No, the envelope was blank, and the note only con-tained the two short paragraphs which I read earlier," Jamal replied unemotionally. As he watched Preston, Jamal noticed Preston's glance at him which Jamal took to mean "go on". Jamal looked down at his lap to gather his thoughts, then continued: "However, there were more pages to the letter, at least two if not more, but these pages had gotten wet, I guess during a rainstorm that afternoon, so by the time I found the letter, those pages had already soaked through to the point they were merged together."

"What did you do with those pages?" Preston inquired.

"I tried to pull them apart, to save what little I could—really, I tried—but it was no use. The pages were disintegrating in my hands even as I tried saving them," Jamal replied with the same unemotional tone which contradicted the substance of his testimony.

"Ah, okay," Preston said as he began pacing in front of the jury. "Now you mentioned a few names when you read the note, what type of involvement or interaction did you have with these people?"

"None, well, none other than Alex, who is my cousin."

"Okay, okay," Preston replied as he nodded for the jury to see. "I'll return to Alex, but first, let's talk about Paige Caruso—how is it that you had no interaction with her? I mean per the note you just read, it seems she worked on the same floor as Audit, so you could have asked her about the note and what she knew."

"I wish I could have talked with her, trust me," Jamal replied sincerely. "Unfortunately, she was no longer with the company by the time I received the letter."

"What happened to her?"

"I don't know, really. When I asked around, no one seemed to know what happened to her. What I heard was, she just didn't come to work; rumor was that she quit suddenly to spend more time with her family."

"Interesting, and this rumor..." Preston started but stopped as he saw Ashlee begin to stand up, ready with an objection. "Now, what about Jayson, the manager mentioned in the note. Was he in the audit department when you joined?"

"No, he was not there," replied Jamal.

"What happened to him?"

"He left South Lake and moved to Denver, where he became Executive VP of Online Sales for Peaked."

"Executive Vice President of Online Sales—sounds fancy. How does that compare to Manager of Audit, or do you not know?" Preston asked, knowing he was walking a thin line and expecting an objection from Ashlee at any moment.

"It is a big step up from Audit Manager, both in terms of salary and career."

"Interesting," Preston said. "And finally, just to be clear, were you involved in any way with the removal of the data from the Peaked and/or South Lake systems?"

"No. As I said, the info was in the thumb drive, which was in the envelope with the letter," replied Jamal al-Bashir. His once full head of short, curly pitch-black hair had slowly begun to turn gray and to thin out, belying his young age; while his neatly trimmed salt-and-pepper beard suited his new older look. This change had begun prior to the trial, but the trial seemed to accelerate the transformation. He was wearing a blue blazer, white button-up shirt with no tie, and khaki pants, all of which hung loosely on his now emaciated body. His youthful appearance at the start of the trial was no more, and his eyes, bordered by black bags, were sunken into his now gaunt face. His once joyful smile had been replaced by an emotionless, permanent parting of his lips, as he breathed air in and out through his mouth. He felt sick, both physically and mentally; something which weeks spent in a crowded jail, fearing what may come next, can do to someone.

"Thank you, no further questions, your honor." Preston Quarles turned away from the podium and walked back to the chestnut-colored wood table on the right side of the courtroom, located in front of the six rows of matching chestnut wood benches completely full of reporters and spectators. Preston worked for a small Charlotte-based law firm that handled mostly civil cases; however, the firm was trying to expand into criminal work, in which Preston had experience, and was why he was recently named a junior partner. He was in his mid-forties, a lush head of reddish hair that he kept swept over his forehead, and he wore his usual beige suit, white shirt, and blue tie. He had a stocky, but not fat build, the result of years of a declining weightlifting regimen that now only saw him in the gym once a week. This was Preston's first trial since being named partner, and he felt the pressure to deliver a great result—not just for his client, who he truly believed was innocent—but also to show the rest of the firm he was deserving of the promotion.

AND CROSS EXAMINATION

"Now Ms. Stallworth, do you have any questions?" asked Judge Eriksson from his elevated seat at the front of the courtroom that allowed him to look down on everyone else.

Judge Eriksson's thinning gray hair, wrinkled face, and thick glasses resting on a thicker nose left little doubt about his age. While his face and neck were pudgy, the rest of his body, which was hidden by his black robe and the wooden table he sat behind, was shockingly thin, the consequence of a strict low-calorie and low-fat diet following two recent heart attacks. He had previously worked as counsel for the Congressional Budget Office and as a Special U.S. Attorney before being appointed to the bench just before the turn of the century. He now found himself counting down the days in dread until his retirement, which was not entirely by choice.

Little did Judge Eriksson know before the start of the trial, but it would be his last. He was dying, not completely, but his mind was, as he had been diagnosed with Lewy body dementia, abbreviated LBD, in the same week Jamal al-Bashir had been arraigned. He had kept his diagnosis secret from everyone, including his ex-wife and two adult children; however, he was feeling its effects set in rapidly, so he formally filed for retirement the day before jury selection. He knew that if he continued and started showing signs, or worse—his diagnosis was made public—it would call into question all the trials he presided over in the past. Years of work for which he was noted and regarded as one of the best circuit judges in the country, undone in a matter of moments by nothing more than sheer speculation and doubt about his abilities.

"Yes, yes your honor" Ashlee Stallworth responded, her wavy black hair covering part of her face as she stood up from her seat. She was dressed in a charcoal pantsuit with a black button-up blouse, and purposely was not wearing any jewelry—a strategy she had employed for all of her trials dating back to her time in the Charlotte District Attorney's Office. She walked gracefully up to the podium that stood between her desk and Preston's, albeit it was a few feet forward of each desk. Ashlee was the same age as Preston, although looked about ten years younger, with her dark complexion and unblemished, smooth skin concealing any signs of her true age. Her path had crossed with Preston's before, as they both had attended Wake Forest Law School, though Ashlee had graduated second in the class while Preston was content finishing with a B average and a considerably lower class ranking.

After law school, Ashlee joined Thatcher Callaghan, a top tier law firm in New York, but quit after one year to work in the Charlotte DA's Office, before eventually moving on to the U.S. Attorney's Office. She had quickly proven herself to be an effective trial attorney and, after only two years, was given the opportunity to first chair

Jamal's trial. She knew that in some part she had been given the case for the better optics—the prosecution of an American Muslim of Sudanese descent by an African American female—but she also believed her assignment was the result of her undefeated record since she had joined the office. And if she were assigned the case to avoid the appearance of racism, she accepted it, as she had her own motives for wanting this case. She knew that the publicity the case was receiving would be just the springboard she needed to launch the next phase of her career. She imagined a run for political office, appointment as a U.S. Attorney or to a federal judgeship, eventually leading to the U.S. Court of Appeals, or—dare she dream—the U.S. Supreme Court. But all of this was dependent upon her winning this case and not making a fool of herself in the process.

"Okay, well then please proceed" replied Judge Eriksson, his raspy voice revealing how worn down he had become during the course of the trial.

"Thank you, your honor," Ashlee said. "Now Mr. al-Bashir, that was quite some story, about some letter you received at random from an unknown person – [pause] – a very, very detailed letter, with dialogue and everything, almost hard to believe that—"

"Objection, your honor, the prosecution is testifying" Preston interjected. "Is there even a question there?"

"Sustained. The government is reminded to keep this to cross examination. You remember what that is, right?" Judge Eriksson ribbed Ashlee with a minor chuckle to let her know he wasn't actually questioning her ability.

"Yes, your honor, will do," Ashlee responded. "Now Mr. al-Bashir, you mentioned earlier that the pay for auditors wasn't great, correct?"

"Um, I might have, I don't think so though. I think I only said I thought I would be doing something else."

"Okay, perhaps, but is it fair to say that you would agree that others at South Lake and Peaked made more than those in the audit department?"

"Yes, I think that is well known in the company and common in the industry, but as I said earlier, I was new to the audit department; I was coming over from accounting, so I can't be sure what was common for auditors." As Jamal replied, Preston closed his eyes and began to rub his forehead in frustration. He knew where this was headed, but also knew he was essentially powerless to stop it.

"Okay, and we will return to your time before Audit, and even South Lake," Ashlee said. "But let's come back to your pay. Is it fair to say you didn't think you earned as much as you should?"

"Objection, relevance," Preston blurted out.

"Your honor, may we approach?" asked Ashlee. Judge Eriksson nodded, and both attorneys approached the bench. Ashlee got a jump on Preston, and immediately argued that her questions were relevant for the purpose of getting to a motive. Preston reiterated that he did not find them relevant. After a brief pause, Judge Eriksson told both attorneys he would allow the questioning but warned Ashlee that she had better get to the point quickly. As both attorneys walked back to their respective locations in the courtroom, Judge Eriksson announced the objection was "overruled".

"Now Mr. al-Bashir, returning to my question" Ashlee started as she shot a quick triumphant glance at Preston before continuing. "Wouldn't you agree that you did not earn as much as you should have?"

"Well, yes, I mean I think most peo—" Jamal began to respond.

"Okay, so you felt you were owed more," Ashlee said, interrupting Jamal. Preston stood up from his seat, but before he could say "Objection", Ashlee continued. "Now, turning to the thumb drive and letter—you said you found them in an envelope, correct?"

"Yes, as I said before, I found the white envelope under a Chinese restaurant flyer on my windshield."

"And when you found it, you did not know who had put it there or what was in it, correct?"

"Yes, when I found it, I had no idea who did it," Jamal replied, annoyed at being asked again.

Ashlee paused for a moment. She debated whether she should press Jamal as to how the envelope came to be on his car's windshield. Part of her felt that, if she kept questioning Jamal about the circumstances surrounding how he found the envelope, the more absurd it would sound to the jury. But then she remembered the first interview the police conducted with Jamal after he was arrested.

Ashlee recalled that during that interview, when the detective questioned Jamal about this very same thing, Jamal stated he thought the envelope was left on his vehicle by mistake. When the detective asked Jamal what he meant by that, Jamal said that he drove a red Toyota Highlander, and there were three other people at South Lake who drove the same vehicle—make, model, and color—who parked in the same employee parking lot. In two subsequent interviews, Jamal offered the same explanation, that he drove a car similar in appearance to at least three other employees who all parked in the same general area. It was a reasonable explanation, and one that was nearly impossible for Ashlee to refute. Rather than risk the chance that Jamal may offer this same explanation again, or that Preston, who apparently had forgotten about the interview, might get Jamal to repeat it on re-direct; Ashlee decided it was best to move on to her next line of questions.

"And there was writing on the outside of the envelope, correct?"

"Yes, there was a note written on it."

"And the note said: 'PLEASE DON'T READ UNLESS I'M DEAD' written in all capital letters, right?"

"Yes, that is what was written on the envelope, along with the other short note taped to the envelope that I read earlier."

"Okay, and despite what was written on the envelope and the note that you mentioned, you decided to open the envelope and read the letter inside anyway, correct?"

"Yes, I did."

"And since you did not know who put the envelope on your car, you had no idea whether they were alive or not, correct?"

"Correct, I didn't know anything about who wrote it or what their status was."

"Weren't you at all suspicious about this envelope, especially the ominous sounding writing on the outside?"

"I was, I mean wouldn't you be?" Jamal replied, the volume of his voice rising, as he was starting to become agitated with Ashlee's questions, and having to repeat what he had said before.

"I'll be the one to ask questions," Ashlee shot back before adding a short laugh as she realized her response was a bit too aggressive. "And now back to my questions." She stopped to direct a small smile at Jamal, intended to be seen by the jury, before continuing: "Despite receiving this suspicious envelope with a note warning you not to read it unless some stranger is dead; instead of going to the police, you decided to read—"

"Objection, your honor, this has been asked and answered already," Preston pleaded.

"Sustained," Judge Eriksson replied.

Preston, watching Ashlee, noticed that she seemed unfazed by the objection, as though she were well past this question. As Preston continued staring, he noticed Ashlee's body shift from standing straight upright to leaning down on the podium and in toward Jamal, as though she were positioning herself to pounce in attack. Preston then turned to look at his client sitting in the box next to the judge's desk. Preston couldn't help but notice how alone his client looked at that moment. He could see the skin on Jamal's face was sunken, and his eyes appeared dull from the exhaustion of testifying. Jamal's cheek bones were visibly protruding, as were the veins on his neck, and his clothes appeared exceedingly loose—all the result of the massive weight loss he had experienced since the start of the trial. Preston knew that if he could see this from his seat, then the jury, who were all much closer to the witness box, saw it as well. Preston turned his gaze away from Jamal and down toward the papers strewn before him on the desk, hoping that the jury did not see him staring. He wasn't sure if his client's appearance would turn off jurors, but he did not want to risk drawing more attention to his client than needed.

"Okay, so Mr. al-Bashir, let's go back a bit. You were an employee with South Lake for seven, no eight years; first in the accounting department and then in audit for only a few months?"

"Yes, that is correct, and I was only in Audit for about two months."

"And Mr. al-Bashir, during that time you were aware of the employee handbook, the code of ethics, as well as other corporate policies regarding employment, correct?"

"Yes, I was, still am, fully aware of them, the code of ethics, employee handbook, and employee policies," Jamal responded. "And you can just call me Bashir, or even Jamal."

Ashlee briefly stopped staring at Jamal and looked up to the ceiling. It was obvious to all watching her that Jamal's response had caught her slightly off guard and she was thinking through what he had said. In a split second, a slight smirk crossed her mouth. Despite being seated adjacent to her and unable to see her full face,

Preston realized that she was smiling at an idea based upon what his client had just said. "Okay, will do Mr. Bashir. Actually, is it that you don't want to be..." Ashlee started but then paused. As she was talking, she realized that her idea, a plan to question Jamal's connection to the late Omar al-Bashir, was not as good as she initially thought. She quickly abandoned the idea and decided to return to her initial questioning.

"Apologies, I lost my train of thought; been a long day, wouldn't you agree? Probably need more coffee tomorrow," Ashlee quipped. Jamal laughed uncomfortably, more a reflex caused by relief than finding her statement funny. He had an idea of what she was going to ask but was thankful she refrained from asking it. "Anyway, so you were familiar with the code of ethics and employee handbook. Would you say you followed it?"

"Yeah, I followed it," Jamal replied.

"And is it safe to assume that during your time at South Lake, you did what your superiors told you to do, as long as it aligned with corporate policies, obviously?"

"Yes, I did what they told me."

"Was that common for you?" Ashlee quickly asked.

"Was what common?" Jamal asked, confused.

"To do what you were told to do. Was that common, not just at work but in life in general, to follow orders, instructions, and the like?"

Jamal paused for a moment as he thought through the question. "Yeah, yes, I believe so," he started. "I think I've always tried to do what is asked and follow instructions."

"Ah, but that isn't completely true, is it?" Ashlee shot back.

"I'm sorry, what, what do you mean?"

"You didn't follow instructions. You said earlier that when you received the envelope it said: "Don't Read, Unless I'm Dead," but what did you do, without hesitation, without waiting to learn if the person who put it on your car was in fact dead—or heck, even finding out if you were the intended recipient. No, instead you immediately opened the envelope and read the letter; you read it despite the note about waiting till the author was dead."

Preston sat patiently listening to Ashlee, giving her some leeway to get to her question, the same as she had given him earlier in the trial. It was this level of professional courtesy which they afforded each other, despite being adversaries, that reaffirmed his appreciation of the legal profession. It might not have been obvious to the general public, but attorneys could at times find themselves being cordial with each other. But as Ashlee continued speaking, Preston felt he could not sit idly by anymore. He first looked over at Jamal, trying to catch his attention, to let him know he should not respond; however, Jamal's eyes were fixated on Ashlee. As she was finishing, Preston stood up with his objection ready, but before he could get the words out of his mouth, Jamal responded.

"Yes, but that was—" Jamal began to say, trying to explain himself; however, he was immediately interrupted by Ashlee.

"And then in terms of South Lake's employee manual,

you knew it said information of South Lake and Peaked were property of each, respectively, and that any info, data, or trade secrets learned were to remain confidential, were not to be disclosed to the public without permission, right?"

"Yes, I knew that, but—" Jamal began again, attempting to abandon his prior statement in hopes of getting out ahead of Ashlee's next question, but he was again immediately interrupted by her.

"But you didn't follow corporate policies, the employee handbook, or the like, did you?" Ashlee asked, raising her voice so as to drown out Jamal's feeble attempt to speak. "No, instead, you published a letter in which you allege details of the internal workings, no doubt trade secrets, of Peaked, and then you released to the world detailed code and algorithms, intellectual property of Peaked, all of which were prohibited by multiple company policies, not to mention the employee handbook and code of ethics, isn't that right?"

"No, it isn't—" Jamal began, but was again interrupted by Ashlee, who had raised her voice to a level just shy of shouting.

"It isn't? So, you're saying you did not release the letter and the codes and algorithms on BlackHat Underground, Corporate Lies Exposed, and half a dozen other message boards and websites?"

"No, I mean...yes, I did, but that wasn't, that wasn't, I mean I didn't do that intending to violate anything. I did it because the public deserved to know," Jamal stammered as he searched for a way to explain what he did without admitting he had violated corporate policies.

"But you did it none-the-less; you released information to the public, although you knew that company policy prohibited you from releasing any proprietary, confidential, or similar information, like trade secrets, isn't that right? You even went further and wrote letters to editors at some of the major national newspapers, hoping to have them publish what you wrote, which included information that only those within Peaked and South Lake, like yourself, knew, correct?"

Jamal reluctantly answered "Yes."

Ashlee then shifted her line of questioning and began cross examining Jamal on specific items from his past. She started off by asking about Jamal's semester-long suspension from his university for cheating. Jamal admitted he had been suspended for a semester after he and some members of his fraternity were accused of cheating on a final; however, the cheating was never proven, and ultimately no one was expelled. Ashlee then began asking about Jamal's working career. She asked about everything from his experience with accounting to the reasons why he spent less than a year at multiple firms, including Booz Allen and The Hartford. Jamal explained the short job stints were a long time ago, before he decided to pursue his master's degree, and before he became more grounded.

While Preston felt strongly that much of Ashlee's line of questioning was not relevant and beyond the bounds of cross examination, he remained seated without objecting. Even after catching two of Judge Eriksson's glimpses on separate occasions where it was clear Judge Eriksson expected an objection, Preston remained steadfast in his approach. He was gambling that objecting too much would hurt his client, as the jury may see it as an attempt to hide something, and Preston saw that Jamal was handling Ashlee's questions surprisingly well, despite some of them being exceedingly uncomfortable. Ashlee then turned her questioning of Jamal to his relationship with Alexander. Jamal freely admitted that Alexander was his cousin, and that Alexander had both helped him to get a job at South Lake, as well as transferring to Audit.

"So now Mr. al-Bashir, if Alexander helped you with these jobs, is it safe to say you two are close?"

"We are family," Jamal replied curtly.

"Yes, yes, we've established that already, but what I want to know, what I want the jury to know is: Are the two of you close?"

"I mean, I guess we are," Jamal started. "We aren't close friends or like that, but yes, we are there for each other and occasionally hang out."

"And when you say you are there for each other, you mean like helping each other out, like with jobs, or school or those types of things, correct?"

"Yes, that is correct, we both help each other out when we can."

"And this helping each other out, that would include how you helped each other to execute this scheme where you profited off of Peaked's stock dropping and stealing information—"

"Objection, argumentative, your honor," Preston said, standing up, his legs wobbling slightly as the blood slowly filtered into his leg after ten minutes of sitting.

"Sustained," Judge Eriksson replied.

"Now Mr. al-Bashir, as you confirmed, you were—sorry, are—close with Alexander? You *are* still close with him, right?"

"I am close with Alex, yes, we always have been close." Preston had advised him about not answering the prosecution's questions immediately to avoid potentially giving an answer before thinking it through. As such, Jamal decided a good method to avoid answering too quickly would be to restate a portion of the question or ask for clarification before giving his answer.

"Great, so now that we've established you two are close, that you helped each other, what I would like to know, what I think this court needs to know is, where is Alexander?"

"I'm sorry, excuse me?" Jamal started.

"It's a simple question: Where is Alexander al-Bashir, your cousin?" asked Ashlee.

"I don't know," Jamal replied, shrugging his shoulders.

"You don't know or you just don't want to answer," Ashlee shot back.

"Objection, your honor," Preston said, standing up cautiously.

"Um, sustained. Ms. Stallworth, um, would you care to rephrase your question," Judge Eriksson said.

"Yes, your honor," replied Ashlee. "Now, Mr. al-

Bashir, is it or is it not true that before the start of this trial, your cousin, Alexander al-Bashir, disappeared?"

"Um, I can't say."

"Can't, or won't say?"

"Can't," Jamal shot back bluntly. He turned his gaze from Ashlee to the jury. While he considered himself far from an expert at reading people, he couldn't help but feel, as he looked at each juror, that they either weren't buying his response, or worse, were upset with it. "I don't know where Alex is. A few days before I found the envelope, I had lunch with him, like we did almost every week. It was our usual lunch. We talked about the Panthers, what they needed to do in the offseason, and then about traveling. He said he wanted to do more this year. But I couldn't help feeling he was maybe holding something back, like something was on his mind but he didn't want to tell me. Anyway, after that I didn't talk to him again. I don't know if he disappeared as you say, or if he just decided to go away on a trip. I can't say because I don't know, but I pray it is the latter." As he spoke, Jamal looked at each juror, trying to glean any indication of how they were reacting; however, they all seemed to be stoic, save for the older female juror on the far left, who visibly rolled her eyes.

"Okay, but isn't it true that before the start of this trial, authorities were looking for Alexander, and that they were unable to find him?"

"You would have to ask whoever these 'authorities' are; I can't say who was looking for whom."

"Alright, fair enough. Well then, if Alexander were

somehow part of this and decided to run, would it be safe to assume that he has gone to the Sudan where you two are—"

"Objection!" Preston shouted across the room as he stood and took four steps toward the podium. "Your honor, the government is asking my client to speculate based on what— random hypothesis? If the government would like to go down this road, then they need to introduce evidence, which they don't have."

"I'm going to sustain the objection, but Mr. Quarles, please just stick to stating your objection; no need to go into exposition in doing so," quipped Judge Eriksson.

"Yes, your honor. Apologies," Preston said, as he retreated to his seat.

With her notepad in her left hand, Ashley then walked around the podium, and toward the jury located less than ten feet from where Jamal was seated in the witness box. When Ashlee was about five feet away from the jury, she stopped, looked down at her notepad, and began flipping the yellow pages over with her right hand. Although it appeared as if she were searching through her notes, Preston knew that was part of her well-rehearsed performance. While most in the room were watching Ashlee, Preston intently watched the jury, and noticed how three members immediately began to lean forward. Perhaps they were curious as to what Ashlee was doing, or they were anticipating what was coming next, or their backs hurt, and they were just re-positioning themselves. Whatever the reason, Preston knew this little performance and pause in the trial was working, as the whole jury was now staring intensely at Ashlee, ready to hear what she had to say next. After about a minute's pause, Ashlee looked at Jamal and then looked at the jury.

"Now Mr. Bashir, isn't it true that you owned shares in Peaked?" she asked, turning her gaze from the jury back to Jamal and then back to the jury as Jamal began to speak.

"Yes, I owned shares in Peaked, that's true," Jamal responded uncomfortably.

"And it wasn't just a few shares, was it? It was, let me see," Ashlee said as she turned away from looking at the jury to glance down at her notepad, then raised her head to look at Jamal. It was 988 shares, totaling over one-hundred thousand dollars, $123,567 to be precise, isn't that correct?"

"It may be. I mean it sounds accurate, but a lot of those shares were through the company's incentive package; they were awarded as part of bonuses."

"Ah, but not all the shares were part of bonuses; you bought a number yourself, right?" Ashlee glanced quickly at her notes and then added: "In fact, you bought over 200 shares yourself, correct?"

"Yes, I signed up for an employee stock purchase plan, which allowed anyone in the company, not just me, to purchase stock at a 5% discount."

"And you had owned these stocks for a long time, since almost your first day at South Lake, correct?" Ashlee then added: "In fact, isn't it true that you had never even sold any shares before this year?" Preston stood up briefly, prepared to object to the double question, when he was interrupted by his own client.

"Yes, that is correct," Jamal said.

"Okay, so here you are, a loyal employee, who has accumulated nearly a thousand shares worth over $100,000 as of the end of last year, and then all of a sudden you are given this envelope with the letter you just read, as well as information about Peaked's A.I. program, and what do you do with the information? You released it to the public, isn't that, right?"

"I felt like I had to release it so that the public knew what was happening" Jamal replied emphatically. "I mean if you were a writer, an artist, a musician, wouldn't you want to know what Peaked was doing, how they were stealing your ideas?"

"Perhaps, and you made the decision to release the info to the public on January 28th of this year, correct?"

"I don't remember the exact date, but yes, that sounds right. I released it because I felt like I was in danger and..." Jamal started while, at the same time, Ashlee began walking back to the prosecution's table. "And that the public needed—"

"And you timed the release of information, so that it came after you had sold off all your stock, leaving you with a nice chunk of money" said Ashlee, interrupting Jamal. A noticeable silence filled the courtroom after Ashlee asked her question. Preston, who was already rubbing his forehead with his right hand, sank down in his chair. Jamal was about to continue his prior statement when the importance of Ashlee's question struck him like a punch to the gut. He sat in the seat motionless as he processed Ashlee's question and how to respond. While it was only a temporary pause, no more than ten seconds, it seemed like minutes to Jamal, who was already exhausted from a day of testifying.

"Isn't that true?" Ashlee pressed, as she stood next to the prosecution's wooden table covered in papers. She leaned over and put her notepad on the table face down and picked up a stack of papers lined up at the top of the table. Preston, who was watching her the entire time, caught a glimpse of two of the red stickers at the top of the papers with the words 'Gov Exhibit 33' and 'Gov Exhibit 34' written on them.

"No, I mean it wasn't like that, I didn't time anything—" Jamal began in reply. As Jamal was talking, Ashlee walked over to Preston's table and showed him the papers. Preston nodded in agreement as he shifted his arms so that his elbows were both resting on the table with his hands clasped almost in prayer. He knew what was coming next and wanted to be fully engaged as, even if he could not stop it, he could at least seem less defeated than if he remained crouched down in his seat.

"No?" Ashlee blurted out while looking back at Jamal and animatedly raising her hands in the air in mock disbelief, in the process interrupting Jamal. "So, you're saying you didn't sell off all your stock before you released Peaked's intellectual property to the world?"

"No, that's not what I said, what I meant was—"

"That is what you were saying, that you didn't time the release of the—" Ashlee started.

"Your honor, objection, argumentative and I don't hear a question," Preston exclaimed as he stood up at the table.

"Sustained. Ms. Stallworth, you are reminded, again, to stick to questions, nothing more," Judge Eriksson chided Ashlee. He didn't typically, if ever, say anything more than "sustained" or "overruled" and definitely avoided admonishing attorneys. However, he could feel himself fading as the day progressed, the pain becoming more noticeable with each moment that passed, which, combined, strained his patience and stoic demeanor. Sitting there, looking down on the courtroom, he just hoped that no one had noticed this change.

"Yes, your honor, my apologies," Ashlee responded in a low, soft voice. "Now Mr. al-Bashir, getting back to the prior question: Is it or is it not true that you published the information on January 28th of this year?"

"As I said, I don't remember the exact date, but I've heard you say it during this trial and that seems probably right, so yes, I guess so."

"And isn't it true that just two days before you released the information, on January 26th, you sold all of your shares in Peaked?"

"Well, it isn't like that," Jamal shot back.

"It isn't like what?" Ashlee began to ask before changing her mind, as she wanted to remain on track. "Never mind that. Now, Mr. al-Bashir, please answer the question: Is it or is it not true that just two days before you emailed almost every major newspaper and put the info about GAIGE online, you sold all your shares, 988 in fact, in Peaked stock?"

"I don't remember the exact date," Jamal began, as a look of annoyance swept over Ashlee's face. Ashlee looked at Judge Eriksson and was about to speak when Jamal added: "But yes, while I don't remember the exact dates, I'm sure you have them, just like all the other dates." After Jamal said this, a brief chuckle from the audience filled the room, and Jamal paused to let the laughter die down before starting again. "And yes, it is true, I did sell my shares in Peaked before I sent the email and put the info about GAIGE online, but I didn't do this as some grand scheme to get rich."

"Oh, you didn't?" asked Ashlee, kicking herself immediately for the question.

"No, the sale of the stock wasn't some scheme," replied Jamal, turning his attention from Ashlee to the jury as he spoke. "I sold the shares because I didn't want to be associated with the company anymore, in any way, after I found out what they did. I also knew that when the story did get out, if I still owned shares in the company, then people would call me a hypocrite and the validity of the details, although true, would be called into question."

Ashlee stood for a moment, squinting her eyes and sucking in her cheeks as she stared blankly in Jamal's direction. After an uncomfortably long pause, she walked back to her table and, with her left hand, picked up two sheets of paper. As she looked back at Jamal, she promptly showed the two new pieces of paper to Preston, who nodded, indicating he had no objection. She transferred the papers from her left hand into her right, which was still holding the other two from before, and then holding up all four papers in her raised right hand, walked back to the witness box and placed the papers on the wooden beam that separated her from Jamal.

"Now Mr. al-Bashir, I'm showing you what has been previously entered into evidence as State's Exhibits 33, 34, 38, and 39. Now looking at Exhibit 33, which we previously established is a stock report for Peaked for the dates of January 26th through February 3rd, what does it say the shares were trading at during that time?"

"Um, it looks like it was trading at between $123.86 and $125.77."

"Pretty consistent price for the week," Ashlee quipped. "Now looking at Exhibit 34, which we've also established is a stock report for February 5th, the day after the story was published in the news, what did the shares close at, not open, close at on that day?

"Um, um, let me see" Jamal stammered as he read over the sheet of paper in his shaking hand. "It looks like the stock closed at $84.13."

"Wow, that is quite a drop in the stock price, right?" Ashlee asked, but before Jamal could respond, continued to her next question. "Now, looking at Exhibits 38 and 39, we previously established these are reports of short positions taken for the weeks of January 26th and February 2nd, respectively. Now as it relates to Exhibit 38, isn't it true that on January 26th, the same day you sold all your shares in Peaked, someone shorted 500 shares of Peaked stock?"

"Well, I'm not an expert at stock reports," Jamal started, as he could feel Ashlee's cold stare. He shifted his eyes to the jury and sensed that his reluctance to answer the question wasn't doing him any favors. "But, but, yes, it does look like someone shorted 500 shares."

"Alright, and now with Exhibit 39, does this indicate how many, if any, shares were shorted on February 3rd, the day before the news story was published?"

"Um, yes, it looks like someone shorted 750 shares on that day."

"So, we've established that the stock dropped roughly $40 per share between when you sold it and the news story broke, and that, during that time 1,250 shares were shorted, which would mean that whoever shorted them would have made roughly $50,000—isn't that correct?

"Yes, I believe so, that sounds about right," Jamal replied reluctantly. From his pre-trial meetings with Preston, he knew to avoid answering questions where he was not an expert; however, he did not think the jury would appreciate the nuances of the different roles and expertise within accounting. Besides, most of this information was already stated earlier during the prosecution's case, and he could not sit there trying to avoid answering the question, pretending as though he did not know what the sheets of paper he held in his right hand said.

Ashlee looked over at the jury trying to catch a brief glimpse of their reaction, which she could not discern, before turning her gaze back to Jamal. She debated whether to continue questioning Jamal about the stock, the timing of the shorted shares, the $50,000 of profits, and such, but decided against it. "No, I can do more damage with what I have now in closing than what I may get from him if I press on now" she thought. She took a few steps to the left, away from the witness stand, firmly placing herself between the jury and Jamal as she prepared her final assault.

"Now Mr. al-Bashir, turning to that day the police arrived at your apartment, isn't it true you threatened them with your gun?" Ashlee started her first volley.

"No, no it is not true," replied Jamal. "When they were banging on my door, I simply said that I had a gun."

"That sounds awfully like a threat. I mean why else would you say you have a gun?" Ashlee questioned. "And isn't it more than that; isn't it true that you yelled at the police, screaming multiple times that you had a gun as you told them to go away?"

"No, I mean... yes, maybe I did yell at them. There was a door between us, so I needed to be loud, so that they heard me, and I probably said it multiple times," Jamal started to ramble before catching himself. He took a brief pause, inhaling, exhaling, and inhaling deeply again. "But it isn't like you are portraying. I wanted them to know I had a gun to avoid violence. I didn't want them busting into the apartment and being surprised by the gun, I did it—"

"Okay, so you yelled at the police about having a gun," Ashlee interrupted Jamal. "And then, when they finally did enter the apartment, they found you, in your office, pointing the gun at your head, ready to fire, isn't that correct?"

Ashlee remained motionless, staring intently at Jamal as she awaited his answer. Behind her, Preston pressed the palms of both hands down on the chair handles, ready to propel himself up to object to what he knew was coming next. Jamal matched Ashlee's stare for a moment, before then looking around the room, first to his right at the jury, then to the left at Judge Eriksson, and finally back at Ashlee. His mouth had gone dry as he mustered the short response: "Yes".

"Now, Mr. al-Bashir, what was the reason why you were intending to shoot yourself?"

"Objection your honor, relevance and speculation," Preston shouted as he sprang up from his seat.

"Your honor, this is highly relevant for what transpired on February 6th, as well as motive; and as for speculation, I think if anyone would know what the defendant was thinking, it would be him. I don't think it is a reach for him to describe his thoughts," Ashlee said without a moment of hesitation. It was clear to Preston that she was ready for his objection with her prepared response.

"Objection overruled," Judge Eriksson said after a short pause. He knew where Ashlee might be going, and was afraid she would push the limit, but despite this and an overwhelming desire to avoid anything that might cause a mistrial, he could not in good conscience sustain the objection at this time. "The defendant is to answer the government's question."

Preston retreated back to his chair, lowering his head,

not wanting to see what he knew was coming next. Ashlee looked over at the jury stone faced, trying everything in her power to hide her emotions, while she awaited Jamal's answer.

"I don't know," Jamal reluctantly said. "It was all sort of a blur, I don't really know what I was thinking."

"You don't," Ashlee said, turning her stare away from the jury and toward Jamal. She took two steps closer to the witness stand before proceeding. "Were you feeling guilt at what you had done, as you knew you were facing forty years in prison—basically the rest of your life—and that is why you were thinking about killing yourself?"

"Objection your honor," Preston screamed as he again sprang from his seat.

"I withdraw my question," Ashlee said before Judge Eriksson could rule. She promptly turned her back on Jamal and walked back to her table. Preston watched her approach and caught a momentary glimpse of a smile. He and she both knew that the damage had already been done just by asking the question.

But Ashlee's temporary joy was quickly replaced by feelings of doubt, regret, and finally anger. For more than ten days she had put forth the best case she had, laying out the evidence — brick-by-brick — to show Jamal was guilty. However, as she stood there that morning facing the jury, she had no clue what they believed. Hell, if she were being truly honest with herself, she probably would not be certain beyond a reasonable doubt of Jamal's guilt either. The entire case essentially rested on two things: whether Jamal was telling the truth about the letter and circumstantial evidence of trading activity, not all of which was even directly tied to Jamal. So, there she found herself, feeling a need to tip the scales in her favor, and resorting to a cheap question she knew was out of line.

When Ashlee reached her table, she picked up her notepad and briefly looked it over, as feelings of regret and anger at her own behavior mounted. Feeling her left hand begin to clench, she took two deep breaths to calm her emotions before she turned back to face the Judge. "I have no further questions at this time."

NIGHTLY NEWS

The main entrance to the long, rectangular two-story building was located on West Trade Street. The building's neoclassical architecture, with faded limestone bricks and columns stood in stark contrast with the modern glass apartment towers that overlooked and overshadowed it. Inside the building was the U.S. Courthouse for the Western District of North Carolina. A small group of people, mostly reporters and cameramen, gathered by the black metal fence located thirty feet from the entrance, and which surrounded the front of the building. One of the people gathered outside was a young reporter who stood facing the camera, with the front of the building behind her in the background. She was in her mid-twenties with short, wavy brown hair, dark complexion, and wearing a red jacket with black shirt and dark blue jeans along with white tennis shoes, which were hidden from view of the audience due to the proximity of the camera lens to her. She held the microphone up to her face as she began to speak.

"Thank you, David—yes it has been quite the day here at the Charles Jonas U.S. Courthouse, in Charlotte, where closing arguments just ended in this highly publicized trial" Jessica Lopez started her report. "However, the real excitement came earlier in the day when the defendant, Jamal al-Bashir, took the stand for the second consecutive day to testify. Between the two days, Jamal al-Bashir spoke for over two hours without any objection from the prosecution, despite the numerous motions and hearings in the weeks leading up to the trial; most of which, according to many sources, were aimed at limiting what information the defendant would be allowed to present in his trial. During the testimony, the defendant read from a letter he claimed to have received, which described how Peaked was allegedly using artificial intelligence, as well as websites they purportedly owned, to steal content from artists that Peaked then generated into its own content for sale on their site. The defendant claimed that this letter was how he came into possession of the confidential information, and after its purported author disappeared, the defendant released the information on discussion websites like BlackHat Underground, as well as submitting it to national newspapers, including the Washington Post and Wall Street Journal, in accordance with the instructions in the letter."

Jessica then paused momentarily to look down at her notes before continuing again. "On cross examination, the government pressed Jamal al-Bashir on the timing of his sale of a large amount of Peaked stock just before he released the information. During closing, the government returned to this, presenting their theory that the defendant was an unhappy employee, who profited from the sale of stock just days before releasing information which subsequently caused Peaked's stock to tumble. In their closing, Jamal's attorney admitted that Jamal had sold his shares before releasing the information but claimed that selling the shares was done out of a desire to get rid of the shares in a corrupt company and argued that the only problematic act was that of Peaked, which the defendant had courageously exposed and now was at risk of being punished for doing so. The case is now with the jury to decide whether they believe that Mr. al-Bashir had been given the information with instructions to release it, or did he do so in a criminal attempt to profit from it."

Jessica stared into the camera lens in front of her face as she listened to David's words on the other end of the earpiece in her ear. As David continued to speak, Jessica nodded her head to indicate agreement as she knew the feed was still live and, while she did not know it, she was being shown on a split screen with David on one side and her face on the other. After David made two statements, she heard him utter the words which clued her in on him asking her a question. She tried to calm her nerves as she readied herself for his question and was already formulating possible responses based on what she anticipated he would ask. When David finished his question, Jessica was filled with relief, as the question was one which she anticipated he would ask, and she began to immediately respond with an answer she had already drafted in her mind.

"That is correct, this case has garnered a significant amount of national attention in the past two weeks. This is in large part due to the publicity generated by Peaked's apparent secretive attempts to keep certain details, including the letter Jamal allegedly received, out of the proceedings—attempts which were made public only recently. With Peaked's supposed interference in the criminal trial, the public has become fascinated by the case which is being seen as a modern-day David versus Goliath, pitting a lonely ex-employee against not just the U.S. Government, but also one of the largest corporations in the world. But another item of note is the geopolitical component of the case. The trial comes at a time when the administration is attempting to repair a strained relationship with Sudan, which deteriorated significantly after last year's kidnapping and murder of three American aid workers outside of Khartoum.

An anonymous source in the administration recently stated the trial of Jamal al-Bashir on insider trading and fraud charges is seen as a major hurdle in the ongoing negotiations with Sudan. This is due to Jamal and his cousin, Alexander al-Bashir, who is suspected of hiding in Sudan, having family connections to Omar al-Bashir, the deposed Sudanese president, who himself was accused and later found guilty of corruption. There is a sense in the administration that the government's prosecution of Jamal and search for Alexander may be seen as retribution, especially by those in the Sudanese government who are still loyal to Omar al-Bashir. Reporting live from Charlotte, North Carolina, this is Jessica Lopez."

THE VERDICT

Jessica stood facing the camera trying to avoid moving any part of her face or body. After about ten seconds, she heard her cameraman state "and we are clear." Upon hearing this, Jessica pulled her earpiece out of her right ear and shifted the microphone from one hand to the other as she slipped off her red jacket. Her cameraman was already back at the large white van with "WTC Channel 4" scrolled across the side. She walked up to the van and placed her microphone inside, as her cameraman continued rolling up the cable that ran from his camera to the inside of the van. Jessica then moved around to the front passenger side, where she placed her jacket on the seat, then checked her makeup in the large side mirror that hung off the door. She was reaching into her back pocket to grab her phone, when her cameraman ran up beside her.

"They reached a verdict," he said while glancing toward the back of the van where the rear doors were still open.

"They what?" Jessica exclaimed. "It's only been thirty or forty minutes."

"I know, but Ken Wilson from Channel 9 came over

and told me they reached a verdict, and the judge is calling everyone back in," he replied.

"Oh, wow," Jessica said. "Okay, well, you get everything set up. I'm going to go inside to see what is going on, and what the verdict is."

"Okay, sure. What do you think this means—guilty or not guilty?"

"Um, oh," Jessica started looking down at her smart watch. "Um, I think it is good for the defendant, so maybe not guilty, but we will see I guess," Jessica said while looking intently back at the courthouse. "Just make sure you have everything set up, and let the studio know we have a verdict, okay" she added.

As the cameraman walked back to the rear of the van to unfurl the cables, Jessica rushed off to the courthouse. She ran across the street and up the steps to the entrance of the building. In that moment, she imagined herself tripping over her heels as she ran up the stairs and missing the verdict. But this thought quickly passed, and she was glad she had decided to wear her white tennis shoes that day instead of heels. As soon as she entered through the glass doors, she saw the crowd of people that had formed just before the metal detector, all waiting to get inside the courtroom. Jessica stood in line, impatiently tapping her phone against her right thigh as she waited her turn. Upon clearing security, she raced across the white marble floor down the hall to the last courtroom on the left, where she encountered the second crowd of people all waiting to get inside.

When she finally did enter the courtroom, she saw

there were no more open spaces in the pews, so she moved to the side wall next to her counterpart from Channel 9. They each gave the other a little smile, but before either could say anything, the bailiff yelled, "All rise". With nowhere to sit, Jessica and those around her remained standing after Judge Eriksson came into the room and sat down behind the bench, at which point everyone in the courtroom, except for those standing by the wall, sat in their seats. Judge Eriksson then asked Ashlee and Preston if they had any matters to discuss or other reason which would prevent calling in the jury, to which both responded in the negative. Judge Eriksson then asked the bailiff to call in the jury, at which point everyone who was seated in the courtroom again stood, blocking Jessica's view of the jury entering the room. When the jury took their seats, Jessica grabbed the little notepad from her back left pocket, where she had kept her notes from the prior three weeks of the trial.

As she had done throughout the trial, she looked over at the defense table where Jamal was seated. She examined him intently, looking for any signs of emotion from him. Just like each of the previous days of the trial, Jamal sat stiffly in the chair, his eyes focused intently on the judge's bench, with no sign of any emotion. Jessica shifted her eyes from Jamal to the first pew located behind the defense's table. She thought back to the start of the trial when she saw Marguerite seated in the first pew, offering words of encouragement to Jamal at the conclusion of each day. As far as Jessica could tell, Marguerite was the closest thing to family Jamal had in the court-room and was the only person supporting him, other than Preston.

However, after the first couple of days of the start of the prosecution's case, Marguerite stopped showing up to court. Today was no different, and Jessica couldn't help but feel some sympathy for Jamal, as in this biggest moment of his life, a moment which may result in him losing his freedom for years, he was sitting alone, without a friend or family member there to support him. Now there were rumors that Marguerite had fled the country with Alex, and was hiding out in France or North Africa, or that, after seeing the prosecution's first couple of witnesses, she had decided that Jamal was guilty. But Jessica chose to ignore all the rumors, as she believed she had some insight on what likely happened.

Before the trial started, Jessica conducted interviews with some of the people who knew Jamal best, including Marguerite. It was the interview with Marguerite which Jessica found most interesting. Marguerite explained how the first time she came to learn about the whole situation was when Jamal called her from jail the day he was arrested. At first, she was in complete shock at the arrest, and then feared what might happen to Jamal as she pictured him in a dirty, cramped jail cell. However, these feelings were later replaced by anger after Jamal told her what he had done. She admitted she was furious at him for acting alone and keeping the whole ordeal a secret from her. But as time passed, she found a way to move on, though not to forgive him.

Like Jessica's other interviews with Jamal's acquaintances, Marguerite swore she did not believe Jamal was guilty. She acknowledged that Jamal was cold and calculating; however, he also lived by a strong moral code. Perhaps more than anyone Marguerite knew, Jamal believed that any wrong acts should not go unpunished. Marguerite sensed that Jamal's perception of justice was formed during his childhood and strengthened over time. Having to live through a brutal civil war, watching his uncle and other family members being accused of horrendous crimes, and then later learning of his uncle's guilt, no doubt had a profound effect on Jamal's sense of right and wrong. He clearly wanted nothing to do with his uncle and tried everything to distance himself from the man. But Marguerite's adamant faith in Jamal's innocence was not what struck Jessica the most during their interview.

When Jessica asked Marguerite about Jamal's relationship with Alex, her attitude noticeably changed. Jessica sensed that Marguerite was irritated by the relationship and may have even despised Alex. Jessica noticed that throughout the interview, Marguerite chose her words carefully, trying to defend Jamal, but at the same time avoided defending Alex. When Jessica asked if Jamal had told her where Alex was, Marguerite replied, "no, Jamal wouldn't tell me, no matter how much I begged him to." The entire conversation with Marguerite left Jessica with the idea that Jamal was covering for Alex and that Marguerite suspected this as well. Jessica believed that it was this notion that strained Marguerite's relationship with Jamal and explained why she stopped coming. No matter how much she loved him, she could not bear watching him taking the fall for someone else.

Jessica pushed the thoughts about her prior interview to the back of her mind. She focused her attention on Jamal, trying to decipher any clues his behavior and movements might offer regarding his emotional state. Jessica moved her eyes back to Jamal and, when Judge Eriksson finally began to speak, she started to scribble down notes as fast as she could, trying not to miss any important facts which she knew she would be expected to report on after the verdict was announced.

"Now, Juror number eight, you are the foreperson, correct?" asked Judge Eriksson.

"Yes—yes, your honor," the thin woman in her mid-forties wearing a white name badge identifying her as 'Juror #8' replied from her seat in the jury box.

"Okay, well, if you don't mind, would you please stand up?" asked Judge Eriksson.

"Yes, sure, sorry, my apologies," the foreperson replied.

"Okay, no apologies needed, it's been a long trial," Judge Eriksson said reassuringly. "Now, I hold here in my hand a jury form, is this form complete?"

"Yes, your honor," she replied.

"And is this verdict signed—I see that it is—is the signature on the verdict form yours?"

"Yes, that is my signature."

"Okay, good. Now that we have that out of the way, have you reached a verdict in this case?"

The woman nodded her head up and down.

"I'm sorry, but would you please answer the question out loud? Our court reporter here, she needs a verbal response for the record," Judge Eriksson said with a slight smile, followed by a wink directed at the juror.

"Yes, I'm sorry, we have reached a verdict," replied the foreperson.

"Okay, well what is your verdict?"

"Umm, ugh, ugh," the foreperson stammered, attempting to clear her throat. "That's better. Okay, we the jury, in the case of United States versus Jamal Ibrahim Hassan al-Bashir, on count one —conspiracy to commit securities fraud and wire fraud — find the defendant guilty."

Jessica's jaw dropped briefly in shock. She quickly turned her eyes from the foreperson back to Jamal, whose head lowered slightly as his gaze shifted from the foreperson to the table in front of him. He remained in this same position, motionless, as the foreperson read out the verdict on the next four charges—guilty on all. As the final count was read, Preston, who was seated to Jamal's left, leaned over and wrapped his arm around him. Jessica watched as Preston began saying something directly into Jamal's left ear, but could not see Preston's mouth moving from where she stood—not that she could read lips, but just to see the expression on his face. She suspected Preston was offering Jamal some words of encouragement, maybe telling him that it wasn't so bad, that they could pursue a new trial, or appeal the verdict. Whatever it was that Preston said to Jamal, it seemed to have no effect, as he remained motionless, his face showing no signs of a reaction.

In that moment, and without any premonition or logical reason, Jessica felt a sudden sickening sense of loss and emptiness. While those around her rushed past on their way out of the courtroom, some to report on the verdict, others just trying to get home, she stood back, pressed firmly against the wall, stricken with these feelings and grappling with what they meant. Three long weeks of trial, of motions, and arguments, and of watching Jamal day-in-and-day-out were now finally over for her, but it wasn't the feeling of elation at finally being done that she would have expected.

No, as she stood, confused as to what was happening to her, she concluded that these nearly crippling feelings sweeping through her body were one half uncertainty and the other half fear. The uncertainty was the simplest to diagnose. She had spent three weeks in this building hearing both sides present their best case, and at the end of all of it, was no more certain of what actually had happened than when she first walked into that courtroom. Fear, yes, that was the feeling she had—it had to be—was much harder to determine. What was its genesis?

It was true she felt in some strange way a connection to Jamal. It was only logical, given the events that occurred. She had spent the better part of fifteen days staring at him for hours on end. But this wasn't the first long trial she had attended, scrupulously watching the defendant for any signs which she could then use in her reporting. Nor was this the first trial in which she had a chance to interview the defendant and those who knew him. Or the first trial where those who knew the defendant claimed he was innocent, incapable of committing the crimes for which he was accused.

But unlike all her prior experiences, this was the first instance where the defendant's emotions never changed, for better or worse, throughout the trial. Even in her interview with Jamal before the trial, he was calm, collected, and emotionless. She could not help but think if the roles were reversed, she would be screaming her innocence, begging anyone to believe her. Instead, Jamal calmly explained what had transpired. She interviewed other defendants, typically murderers, in the past who also calmly explained everything. What separated Jamal from these other men, most of whom she suspected were sociopaths, was that she believed him. When she asked if he had any regrets, Jamal said he had many, but none more than the pain and anguish he had put Marguerite through. Jessica asked him at the end of the interview if he thought it was all worth it. Jamal simply responded, "I don't know, I stopped asking myself that days ago, there's no point anymore."

This was also the first trial Jessica had covered where those who had known the defendant for years admitted in their interviews to not really knowing who he was. If she had to summarize the most common refrain she heard, it would be "I've known Jamal for X years, but I'm sorry, I don't really know him, we never spent much time together." If she had to guess, she would say that outside of his cousin and Marguerite, Jamal didn't have a friend in the world. And here he was, on the verge of going away to prison for the better part of the rest of his life, and he was all alone in his greatest time of need.

"Ma'am, ma'am," said a male voice. "I'm sorry, but we are closing the courtroom for the day."

"What...," Jessica began, snapping out of her rumination.

"Sorry, but we are closing the room, if you wouldn't mind making your way out," said the older man in his mid-sixties.

"Oh, yes, sorry," Jessica replied as she placed her notepad in her back pocket. She proceeded to walk out of the room, then out of the building and toward the white WTC Channel 4 van. As she approached the van, her cameraman jumped out of the driver side and stood facing her.

"So, what was the verdict?" he asked.

"Guilty, guilty on all counts," Jessica replied as looked back at the courthouse. Turning back to her cameraman, she asked "hey, do you have a cigarette?"

"A cigarette," he replied, a bit flabbergasted. "Um, yes, but I didn't think you smoked."

Reaching her hand to take a cigarette from the little red and white pack he had pulled from his hip pocket, she replied "I don't".

MEET AND GREET

The short man wearing a white button-up and dark blue blazer stood in the parking lot checking his phone for any recent messages. "Where is he?" he wondered when he looked up to see a car pull into a nearby spot. He watched as a tall, pudgy man wearing a pink polo with pullover exited and walked over to him.

"Hi Geoff," the man said, walking up anxiously.

"Hey Richard," Geoff responded. "You ready to do this?"

"Um...," Richard stammered then paused to look down at his shaking hands.

"Look, it will be alright, just do as we talked about, okay?" Geoff said reassuringly. He watched Richard, who seemed still preoccupied with his shaking hands. Geoff sighed and began to worry that this was not a good idea. "Alright, well, let's go do this thing," Geoff said, turning to walk toward the building. "You coming?"

"Huh?" Richard asked, looking up to see Geoff walking away from him. "Oh, yeah, sure, I'm coming."

The two men walked up to the thick wood door of the one-story building. Geoff stopped and looking over at Richard, noticed the tiny beads of sweat forming along the ridge of his scalp. Geoff sighed and shook his head, then felt the inside of his coat before finally opening the door. They walked into the dimly lit room, the stale air smelling of old, spilled beer. Looking to the left of the bar at the center of the room they saw a man sitting at the last table in the far back of the room, past the dart boards and arcade games.

"Is that our guy?" Geoff inquired discreetly.

"Yes...Yes, that's him!" Richard shouted. Geoff shook his head again in disappointment. It was not that loud in the bar, but obviously his companion was nervous and struggling to calm himself.

When they walked up to the table, the man stood up defensively, seemingly ready to flee if needed. Geoff looked him over from head-to-toe. The man was on the taller side and had a thick beard. He was wearing a black baseball cap with an American flag patch on the front and had on a large, equally black hoodie. As Geoff was sizing him up, he sensed that the man was doing the same to him. No doubt the man had come to the conclusion he had—that the man had a significant size advantage over him.

"Hey, you're late!" the man exclaimed with a gruff voice. "Is this the guy?"

"Hi, yes...yes," Richard stammered. He placed his shaking hands in his pant pockets, trying to hide them before continuing, "Robbie, this is Geoff."

"Hey, how's it going?" Geoff said, extending his right hand out toward Robbie.

"Hey," Robbie replied, shaking Geoff's hand before

settling back down in the seat at the table. "So, Rich tells me you have a little job you want to get done, eh?"

"Yes, that's right," Geoff replied, as he sat down as well.

"Alright, well, before we get started, you want anything to drink?"

"Um, I guess we'll have whatever you're having," Geoff replied, looking over at Richard who was staring down at the table. Then added "On us of course."

Robbie looked over at the bar and caught the attention of the man behind it. Robbie pointed to his empty glass and then raised four fingers. The bartender nodded and quickly walked over with three glasses filled halfway up with a brown liquid.

"Hope you boys like Jameson," Robbie said as he lifted one glass and gulped down its contents.

"Of course," Geoff stated, taking a sip from the glass. "Now, I take it Rich filled you in a little on what's going on?"

"Yup," Robbie replied. "Well, he told me he has a little problem, but I don't see where you come in on this."

Geoff looked over at Richard who was now looking up from the table. He could see the sweat was now dripping down the back of his neck. "Shit!" he thought. Geoff turned his gaze back toward Robbie while he simultaneously kicked Richard in the leg under the table and out of sight of Robbie.

"Ow—" Richard started to cry out before collecting himself. He cleared his throat before starting again.

"Geoff here is, um, he owns a contracting firm in Winston-Salem and is, um, um..." Richard began to stutter.

"I'm also a silent partner in Richard's firm, although we don't like to advertise that," Geoff interjected. "So, we have the same problem—Mathis Construction."

"Okay," Robbie said, nodding his head. "And you want something done with this Mathis fellow? Something that, well—that takes him *out of the picture*, so to say."

"Yes, that's it," Geoff replied. "You see, this guy, he's got some connections who make sure he wins nearly every contract. And he's done this across the state. Essentially, when he comes to town, he drives all the competitors out of business. So, you can see our concern and why we want something done."

"Gotcha, yeah, that might be something I can help you guys with," Robbie said with a grin as he leaned back in his seat.

"Now, before we proceed, I was just wondering, I mean do you have experience with this sort of thing?" Geoff asked, looking around the room.

"Oh yeah, I got a lot of experience with this," Robbie boasted with a laugh. "I've *taken care of* people all up and down the South—from Tampa to Baltimore. For example, there was the young, blonde wife in J-Ville who wanted her older, rich husband dead so she'd inherit his fortune. Then there was this guy in Atlanta who wanted to leave his wife for his trainer but didn't want to lose half his stuff to the wife in divorce." Richard looked over in disbelief at Geoff, who was unfazed and listening intently to Robbie.

"Oh, then my favorite—Orlando. This wife learned

her husband was having an affair with their twenty-something babysitter and—needless to say—she was furious. The wife hires me and says she wants him to suffer. So, one day she goes out to meet a bunch of friends at lunch while her husband stays behind. Well, I had snuck into the house earlier that morning and waited upstairs for a couple hours. Eventually he comes upstairs to get something and as he's standing at the top of the metal staircase about to walk down, I rush up from behind and push him. He tumbles down, hitting every other stair, before he lands at the bottom. I ran down the stairs and found his neck was broken—he can't move—but is still alive. I grabbed a picture off the wall and used the edge—you know so the bruise looks like it came from a stair—to push down on his chest, slowly pressing the air out of him. Within a few minutes he's dead and it looks like he tripped while coming down the stairs."

"Interesting," Geoff said leaning back in his chair. "But you see, what we want is a little bit different. We don't just want him out of the picture; we also need to get some information. Like who his contacts are and maybe whatever dirt he has on people that allow him to keep winning these bids. We need to know who he's talking to, what info is being exchanged, etc., before he is *taken care of*. Basically, corporate espionage type thing. I don't suppose you have any experience with that sort of thing?"

"Ha," Robbie chuckled. "Yes, I think you could say I have experience with that sort of thing." Before Geoff could ask for an example, Robbie began bragging again. "Just a few months ago I was hired by this *large* company back in Charlotte to look into some employees suspected of stealing company information. I followed a few of them around for weeks, tracking everything they did and everyone they met with. I also searched their homes and cars. I learned this one employee was indeed getting company info he shouldn't have and he was spreading the info around. Obviously, the company wasn't happy and wanted something done about it, but it had to be quiet."

Robbie leaned forward in his chair and looked around the room before continuing. "Well, I knew from following the guy he was a morning runner. So, one morning I camped out on this park bench on this running trail I know he uses. I hear him coming down the path at the usual time and I sit down on the path clutching my chest and moaning. He runs up and thinks I'm having a heart attack or something and he offers to help me. I tell him I need to sit on the bench. While he's focused on holding me up and getting me to the bench, I pull out my gun, place it in his mouth and bang! He falls backwards and onto the bench and I place the gun in his right hand. I then place a short, typed suicide note in his left hand. And to top it all off, the day before this, I entered his car while he was at work and hid a receipt for the gun I purchased with cash in the glovebox. Police weren't even at scene more than thirty minutes before they ruled it a suicide."

"Amazing," Geoff exclaimed. "And you said there were other people you were following around as well?"

"Yeah, there was this redhead who was friends with the park bench guy and came across some info after I *took care of* the park bench guy. I drugged after she left the gym one night and then dumped her in a nearby lake and made it look like she left the area to be with family out west. Then there was this other person, an accountant or auditor or something, who was doing some internal review and was becoming a problem. I ended up having to knock him out, injected him with a shit load of meth and then placed him in an abandoned building known to be used by junkies. I actually heard the building recently burned down. Oops!" Robbie chuckled as he shrugged his shoulders. "Anyhow, does that answer your question?"

"Yes, yes it does," Geoff responded.

"Great, now to business," Robbie said leaning forward in his seat. The grin he had while telling stories of his past murders was replaced by a stern expression. "So, based on what you're telling me, my fee is $35,000 flat.

"Thirty-five thousand?" Richard blurted out as he placed his drink back on the table.

"Yes, thirty-five and that's non-negotiable, okay?" The two men across from Robbie both nodded in agreement. "And that will be ten upfront now, another ten in two weeks, and the final fifteen upon completion of the job, got it?"

"Got it," Geoff answered. "Thirty-five total to get information on and then kill Jonathan Mathis, right?"

"Yes, that's what I said," Robbie replied, annoyed with having to repeat himself. "And ten is due now, not 'now' like tomorrow or next week, I mean now, right here, no delay. You do have it right?"

"Yes, of course," Geoff said as he reached into his coat

pocket. He then pulled out an envelope and placed it in the middle of the table. Robbie grabbed the envelope and briefly looked at its contents before placing it in the pouch on the front of his hoodie. Robbie then motioned to the bartender to bring over four more drinks. As the bartender was approaching the table, Geoff felt a buzz in his coat and pulled out his phone. He rotated the screen, so it was out of Robbie's view and read the message: "We got it all. Moving in now, be ready." The bartender placed a drink in front of Geoff when he caught a glimpse of Geoff's phone and the message on it. While Geoff shifted his body weight in the seat, he missed the bartender mouthing a word to Robbie before the bartender walked back to the bar. Robbie sat for a moment wondering what to do next.

"So, Geoff, how do you do it?"

"Hmm," Geoff muttered. "How do I do what?"

"How do you manage to run your own business, be a silent partner with this guy," Robbie replied while pointing over at Richard. "And…then find time for a busy police schedule?"

Geoff felt a shock run through his body as his heart rate jumped. "Shit" he thought. He looked down at his chest as he reached into his coat. As he grabbed the handle of his gun, he looked up and saw the glittering object approach his face. Geoff immediately fell backwards when the glass struck him in the face. Robbie leapt out of his seat and rushed to the door. He paused momentarily to look back at the table where Geoff was now kneeling on the floor, blood gushing from his cheek and bent nose.

Pleased with the sight, Robbie pushed open the heavy door and stumbled out of the bar. Once outside, he heard it.

"Freeze, don't move, this is the police!"

A GOOD APPEAL

Preston sat back in his plush, padded leather chair. He put down the 150 plus page transcript and looked out the window. From his office on the twenty-fifth floor of the 400 South Tryon tower he could see the small Romare Bearden park and the adjacent minor league baseball field. The Charlotte Knights players were taking the field, likely a pre-game warmup. "I didn't know there was a game tonight—I wonder if I should get tickets?" he thought. It would be a good, and much needed, distraction from what he was doing.

Seven weeks had passed since the guilty verdict was announced in Jamal's case. In the time between, Jamal was sentenced to forty years in federal prison, and Preston's motion for a new trial was denied. Now, Preston found himself poring over countless pages of trial transcript, pieces of evidence, and legal cases as he prepared Jamal's appeal. With each day he sat down to draft the appeal, he found himself playing Monday-morning-quarterback with the trial.

"So many missed opportunities," he thought each time he read and re-read the transcript. He kicked himself for not asking Jamal why he thought the note was placed on his windshield. "That Jamal drove the same make, model, and color of vehicle as three other employees at South Lake was exactly what the jury needed to hear," Preston said to himself, although, it would have only been Jamal's word. The police never investigated if anyone else at South Lake drove a red Highlander, and Preston received no help when he asked around—something that happened too much with this case. There was also a good chance that Ashlee would have objected on grounds of speculation, but it was a chance he had needed to take and missed. And there were many more examples where he felt he could and should have done better.

Preston's thoughts then turned to his last encounter with Jamal. They had met in the small, windowless room at the Mecklenburg County Jail where Jamal was temporarily being held until his final federal penitentiary was assigned. Preston remembered how Jamal seemed more interested in talking about Charlote FC's season and the star wide receiver the Panthers had signed than his appeal. What struck Preston most was how unfazed Jamal seemed to be with what was happening to him—just like every other time they had met. Preston knew through conversations with Marguerite, who paid for Jamal's defense, that apathy was just part of his personality. But Preston believed there was something else there.

In their pre-trial conversations, Jamal seemed resigned to being found guilty and going to prison. While Jamal professed that Alex was innocent, he gave off the impression he knew where Alex was but was not going to tell anyone. Jamal did not even bat an eye when Preston mentioned Ashlee's offer to plead guilty, sentenced to ten years with five to serve and tell authorities where Alex was. Preston got the sense that Jamal felt it was his obligation to go to prison, rather than cut a deal in exchange for betraying his cousin, who meant so much to him and to whom he felt he owed so much.

With the trial over and the hope of freeing his client fading, Preston felt it was finally time to ask. Sitting in that room across from an apathetic Jamal, Preston questioned Jamal why he had not been more vocal and passionate about his innocence at the trial. Jamal calmly replied, "I knew they were going to find me guilty, one way or the other." When Preston asked how he could be so certain, Jamal explained that Peaked needed "a body" and they were not going to stop until they got one. "Who better than the man who leaked the secrets to serve as the scapegoat," Jamal added. Preston tried to explain that it did not have to be so black-and-white, and he could have fought harder or taken a deal. Jamal replied that neither of those choices was an option. Preston vividly remembered as their meeting came to an end, Jamal's final words to him, "At least now that they have their guy, they won't be looking for Alex—his freedom, his safety, that's all that matters."

Preston tried to re-focus on the present, as he watched the players in the stadium below stretch and then jog about the outfield. The sun had begun its initial, slow descent into the horizon. He wanted to keep watching the players below but the light from the setting sun was becoming too much for his sensitive eyes. He looked back at his desk piled high with papers and debated whether to continue working on the appeal or call it a day and grab a quick drink at Valhalla Pub before the game. "You probably could get two drinks at Valhalla for what one at the stadium would cost," he told himself. That was all he needed to tell himself, before deciding to turn off his laptop. He was in the middle of scrolling through his text messages, ready to see if anyone wanted to join him for a drink when his office line rang.

"Hey, Patrick, unless this is urgent, I was about to head out," he said.

"Oh, sorry, well I have a call here for you—do you want me to say you've left for the day?" asked the young male voice on the other end.

"Um, well who is it?" Preston asked, annoyed at having to ask his secretary this simple question.

"Oh, yeah, sorry—Ms. Jessica Lopez," responded Patrick.

"Okay, well that doesn't ring a bell," Preston said, rubbing his right fingers across his eyes in frustration. "Did she say what she wants?"

"Um, no, no I don't think so," Patrick replied.

Preston could feel his frustration and anger mounting with each of Patrick's responses. "Typical millennials," Preston thought to himself. He sat for a few seconds trying to decide what to do next, as part of him had already checked out for the day and was ready for drinks and baseball. But his innate curiosity won over in the end. "Okay, well, put her through."

"Hi, Preston, this is Jessica Lopez with Channel 4 news," the young female voice said.

"Hi, Jessica, how can I help you?" Preston nervously responded. In his experience, reporters never called with good news. Typically, it meant one of his clients had done something awful and the reporter was trying to get a comment.

"Actually, I may be able to help you," she replied.

"Oh, really, how so?"

"It's about Jamal," she replied. "There are some recent events that may help him...help you with his appeal."

"Um, alright, well what do you mean by recent events?" Preston asked.

"There's been an arrest," Jessica shot back. "Look, sorry I can't say more, I'm about to go on the air. Just tune into Channel 4, okay?"

The line went dead before Preston could say anything. It was a strange call to say the least. Preston had never received one like it before in all his years of criminal defense. He looked down at his watch, which showed the time as 4:56 pm. Preston stood up from his chair and walked out of his office down the hallway to the large conference room. There, he turned on the television mounted on the side wall and sat down at the long table. Using the tablet built into the table, he scrolled through the channels till he arrived at Channel 4.

He watched the television as it cycled from one medication related commercial to another. "I never realized how ridiculous some of these drug names are," he thought to himself. After a couple minutes, Preston saw the familiar nightly news graphics flash on the screen, followed by the introductions of the two co-anchors. Each anchor took turns previewing the stories they were going to discuss over the next half-hour. After this, the lead female anchor introduced the first story of the night.

"We begin tonight with the recent arrest of a man in Greensboro for solicitation to commit murder and assault on an officer. We are learning now that this suspect has now been linked back to at least three other deaths in the Charlotte region in the past few months. Our very own Jessica Lopez has been following this story closely over the past twenty-four hours and is reporting live from Greensboro tonight."

"Thank you, Diane. I am standing outside the Kilkenny Pub here in downtown Greensboro, where less than 48 hours ago the police made an alarming arrest that resulted in one officer being hospitalized. In a scene that could have been lifted straight from *The Sopranos*, an undercover officer met with a Keith 'Robbie' Bukoski, around 8:30 pm. During this meeting, the officer solicited Mr. Bukoski to murder someone, which the suspect allegedly agreed to do for $35,000. Before the officer could arrest the suspect, he allegedly struck the officer in the face with a glass before finally being taken into custody."

Preston yawned as he looked down at his watch. If he left now, he could still get in one drink before the game started.

"The suspect was subsequently charged with one count of solicitation to commit murder and assault on a law enforcement officer. But in a startling turn of events, I've learned from multiple sources, who wish to remain anonymous due to the ongoing nature of the investigation, that this may not have been the suspect's first foray into murder. These sources told me that suspect is now under investigation for the possible murder of Nicholas Stern, as well as a few others, who have not been named yet."

Preston's heart immediately began to race when he heard the last part. "Could it be?" he asked himself. He looked out the large windows facing the nearby apartment as Jessica's report continued. "Now we at Channel 4 are still trying to gather more information about the suspect, but what we do know is his name is Keith Robinson Bukoski, aged 38, of Raleigh. He is a veteran who deployed twice—once to Iraq and another time to Syria. After he left the Navy, he moved to Charlotte, where he apparently worked numerous jobs, including at a local gym and as a bouncer at some local bars."

Preston desperately tried to recall the contents of the letter Jamal claimed to have found. He rushed out of the conference room and down the hall back into his office. He sat in his chair trying to gather his thoughts. He knew what he had to do next but was unsure what he would even say. Taking his phone out from his pocket, he briefly scrolled down the list of contacts till he saw her name— ASHLEE STALLWORTH. Taking a deep breath, he pressed the little blue phone icon, turned on *Speaker*, and placed the phone on the desk.

LET'S MAKE A DEAL

"Hello Ashlee, this is Preston Quarles," Preston began when the ringing stopped, and he heard the little beep indicating someone had answered. "How are you doing?"

"Preston, oh hey, how is it going?" Ashlee responded with a sound of surprise. "I—I was going to give you a call tomorrow, actually."

"Ah" Preston replied before pausing to think about how he would proceed. "Perhaps I've saved you the call then. I was calling you about the arrest of Daniel Bukoski the other night in Greensboro—are the Feds aware of this? Are you guys going to be involved?"

"Um, well, you know we don't comment on pending cases, especially local PD cases," Ashlee replied. Preston could tell she was stalling.

"I know, but I'm not looking for an official comment, just whatever info you may have," Preston asked. There was a moment of silence on the other end of the line. Feeling desperate, Preston pleaded, "Look, I don't want to put you in an uncomfortable position, but I'm working on Jamal's appeal, which is due Friday, so any info you can give would be a great help." Another, longer moment of silence followed. "And I know you have no interest in seeing my appeal succeed, but if there is any information relevant to this case, the Government has an obligation, a duty to provide it."

"Okay, okay," Ashlee finally replied. "Alright, so this is still under investigation, okay, meaning you can't hold me to this, but this is what we know so far. The Greensboro PD learned of someone offering murder-for-hire services in town. A joint task force was formed between Greensboro PD, CMPD, North Carolina Bureau of Investigation, whereby an undercover Greensboro PD officer arranged a meet-and-greet at a local bar with an individual named Daniel Bukoski. Now, during this meeting, the officer asked Bukoski about his experience in this area." Ashlee paused for a moment, seemingly for dramatic effect before continuing.

"Well, it turns out, this Bukoski guy is quite the talker, although probably not the brightest. He started bragging about murders he committed all over the Southeast. Now, much of what he said may just be made-up stories trying to over-sell his qualifications. But as he kept talking, he disclosed details of two people he claimed to have killed in Charlotte—details which were not made known to the public—which caught the attention of CMPD officers who were monitoring the conversation. One of the people he mentioned killing was Paige Caruso, a former South Lake Union employee, who was missing and whose body was recently recovered from Lake Norman."

"Wait a minute," Preston blurted out. "How can that be? I didn't even know Paige was missing."

"Apparently, other than a sister in Arizona she didn't speak with much, Paige didn't have any close family members," Ashlee said. "And all her friends in Charlotte thought she moved to the West, so no one reported her missing till just the other day—right before they found her body."

"So, you're saying he killed Paige and Nick, two people who were mentioned during the trial?"

"Yes, and that's not even half of it. So, get this, just an hour after Bukoski is booked, he tells the detectives he's willing to make a deal. Curious, the detectives ask him what he would have left to offer to make a deal. He tells them he's willing to tell them about other murders and, more importantly, who hired him to commit them. So, I'll spare you the details of the deal that was worked out, but afterwards Bukoski starts talking. He tells the officers that he was contacted about eight months ago by Dominic Simon, whom he served with in the Navy. Dominic, who now was a mid-level executive at Peaked, starts off with some small talk, chatting about their old Navy days, but as the conversation progresses, Dominic asks what Bukoski is doing and how he is getting by these days. Bukoski senses that Dominic wants more than to just catch up.

The conversation leads to them arranging to meet in person a few days later, at which time Dominic asks Bukoski if he would want to get paid to follow some people around and report back to him. Bukoski agrees and for the next month or so starts following a couple of people around Charlotte. This then leads to Bukoski agreeing to intimidate these people. He said the intimidation was harmless at first, mostly driving close behind them and tapping on their windows or doors. But soon Dominic was asking for more and more, till the point when Dominic finally asks if Bukoski would be willing to 'make someone disappear.' Bukoski understood this to mean only one thing—murder. He agrees to murder the first person, Nicholas Stern, which he staged to look like a suicide. Dominic then asks him to 'take care of' at least three other people. One of them was Paige Caruso. Another person, who you may find especially interesting, was an auditor at South Lake, who was reported missing by his family last November, right about the same time Jamal claimed he received the letter and thumb drive."

"Wow, just wow," Preston said in dismay.

"Yup, and guess what he drives?"

"A metallic blue Mustang."

"Yup, you got it," Ashlee happily answered. "We even found some personal items—a credit card, photo, and gym bag—belonging to these people in Bukoski's trunk, of all places."

"Wow," Preston repeated, still astonished with what he just heard. As he ran his fingers through his hair, his mind was flooded with questions. Figuring Ashlee would soon need to go, he had to choose his next questions wisely. "So, who is this auditor that Bukoski claims to have killed?"

"Oh, well, it doesn't look like that is a claim anymore," Ashlee started. "He provided details which we believe links back to a recent unidentified body found in an abandoned, burned down home."

"Interesting, and does this person have a name?"

"I'm sorry, we can't release that yet as we are still waiting on DNA testing and then obviously have to tell the family."

"Okay, that makes sense," Preston replied with a hint of annoyance in his voice. "And what about this Dominic, is there anything you can tell me about him?"

"Yes, but again, this is off-the-record, so don't hold me to anything. A few hours after Bukoski gave up Dominic's name, FBI agents in Denver arrested Dominic. Much like Bukoski, this Dominic guy seemed more than willing to talk for a deal, and a couple hours ago gave a full statement. Dominic stated that he was approached by Frederik Raburn, Peaked's Head of Online Sales, last October. Apparently, Dominic was helping Raburn manage some of the money transfers related to GAIGE. Raburn stated he was concerned a recently uncovered embezzlement scheme may bring some unwanted attention. As such, Raburn explained he commissioned an internal investigation to determine how well they had concealed the funds being diverted in and out of the GAIGE account.

Raburn then stated he suspected there may be a company mole and asked Dominic to investigate. Dominic reached out to some of his old Navy buddies, including Bukowski, to start surveilling some suspected Peaked and South Lake employees. This surveillance soon progressed into increasingly more aggressive tactics at the behest of Raburn. Dominic then told agents that when Raburn learned Nick was leaking info about GAIGE, Raburn told Dominic to 'make sure he's not around to do it again.'

Dominic claims that Raburn gave a similar order when he learned that this auditor was looking into GAIGE." Ashlee started coughing. "I'm sorry, would you excuse me for a moment?"

"Yeah, of course," Preston answered. He felt a sudden exhilaration and surge of enthusiasm. He had been at a loss with Jamal's appeal and this new information gave him renewed confidence that they had a chance. He wanted to start working on the draft as soon as possible but also realized he needed to tell Jamal the good news. While Ashlee's coughing fits continued in the background, Preston pulled up his calendar. There were two client meetings in the morning, but he could afford to cancel them both, as he wanted to talk with Jamal as soon as possible. Preston was typing the email canceling his 9:30 am meeting when he heard Ashlee's voice.

"Sorry about that," she said. "I don't know what came over me. Nevertheless, I need to go soon."

"Oh, yes, of course," Preston said, looking down at his watch which now showed 6:12 pm. "Thank you so much—this should be a huge help with the appeal."

"No problem, but look, you know this doesn't change anything. I still think your guy is guilty and I'm going to oppose your appeal. But... I think there is probably enough here to warrant a new trial and from there it is up to the jury to decide, unless a deal is reached before then."

"Yes, I understand, I know you have to do what you have to do," Preston responded, ignoring her attempt to coax a discussion about a potential plea deal. "So, then,

I guess we'll see each other in court again?"

"No, probably not," Ashlee replied. "If a new trial is granted and if my boss decides to re-try the case, it will probably be assigned to some junior attorney."

"Oh," Preston said with a hint of disappointment in his voice at hearing he would not get a second chance to beat her. Preston then jokingly asked "You sure you don't want to go through all that fun again?"

"I'm sure," Ashlee responded with a chuckle. "Besides, I know a loser case when I see one. Talk soon, bye."

"Of course, bye," Preston replied just before the line went dead.

He sat back in his chair dumbfounded by what he had just heard. The whole story seemed almost impossible to believe. Preston looked aimlessly out the window ruminating on the implications of what Bukoski's confession meant to the case. Unlike Ashlee, Preston was not entirely sure the new details guaranteed a new trial, let alone Jamal's freedom. But one thing was for certain: the baseball game could wait till another day. Preston finally had what he lacked at trial—evidence proving Jamal had not fabricated the entire story.